HER CALLING

Book One of New Beginnings

Kaden Shay

Supposed Crimes LLC • Matthews, North Carolina

All Rights Reserved
Copyright © 2020 Kaden Shay

Published in the United States.

ISBN: 978-1-952150-11-1

www.supposedcrimes.com

This book is typeset in Goudy Old Style.

HER CALLING

CHAPTER ONE

THE SOUNDS *of labored breathing, hitching here and there with the soft brush of skin on skin, the sweep of tingles and the shuddering twitch of muscles that followed. Fingers drift lightly across arms, shoulders, chest, stomach and legs, barely more than a flutter over the surface, but sending each nerve ending into overdrive. Arousal heightened, flushed skin and a quickened the rush of blood to already sensitive body parts that screamed for attention. Breath teased and tickled down silky flesh, chilling over a thin coating of fresh sweat, ripping a gasp past parted lips. A tongue darting out momentarily, wetting full lips with a shine of moisture as heavy lids slide closed over ice blue irises.* Just as things took a turn for the very best and started heating up even further, a shrill screeching stopped it all dead.

I grumbled and slapped at the alarm clock on my bedside table, growling at the damned thing for cutting off the best dream I'd had in weeks. Ever since my last secret meeting with a member of the neighboring pack I'd been sneaking around with for the last two years, I'd been plagued by dreams that never quite got where I hoped they would. That meeting had been cut short when my father's scouts had ventured a little closer to our meeting place than they normally did. Neither of us had managed to find the time for another rendezvous since then and that had been over six weeks ago. That fact was painfully obvious just then as I rolled over, threw off the covers and instantly felt the need for a very cold shower.

A huff escaped me as I rubbed my eyes with the backs of my hands to clear them of the morning gunk that always plagued me and then I sat up and stretched my arms toward the ceiling for a good shoulder pop before I slid out of bed. My bare feet hit the wood of the floor, cold from being exposed to the northern November air all night. I shuddered a little bit and then smiled as the chill spread over my still far-too-warm body, helping to ease the heat the rather realistic dream had left in its wake. I sighed heavily, shook my head and then headed across the room to the bathroom, bare feet making no sound on the smooth, polished floor. After I stepped in and flipped on the light, I swung the door closed, sealing off the small room to keep whatever heat might build up in the space trapped.

I turned the shower on, electing for a typical warm wash thanks to the chilled air having relieved most of the ache that had settled itself annoyingly in my lower body. After adjusting the knobs a little, I turned to look in the mirror over the sink and made a face at myself. My typically-tamed strawberry-blond hair was a mess, looking very much like I had actually engaged in the carnal acts that had slipped through my dream-world. I growled a little at my reflection, let my nose wrinkle some and pulled the left side of my upper lip up just slightly, despite the fact that it wasn't a very attractive gesture. Steam started to rise from the shower, catching my attention so I let the expression fall back into a more flat overtone. After a last little huff, I turned away from the mirror, stripped off the tank top and shorts I normally slept in and stepped into the shower, wincing as the water hit my now cooler skin for the first time. I realized that I might have let it get a little hotter than I'd been meaning too. Oh well, my skin would settle in and get used to it after a couple minutes, no use messing with it any further.

I took the few minutes I normally needed and washed up, shut off the water and grabbed a towel, drying off as I left the bathroom, a spattering of goose bumps rippling over my bare body the instant the colder air of the bedroom hit me. I couldn't help but smile at the delightful change in temperature and let the wet towel fall to the floor as I headed over to the dresser against my wall. After digging through a couple drawers, I settled on a slightly-newer matching set of underwear, black with a shock of teal edging to it, I loved teal. Fighting the stubborn bra took a minute but once it was in place, I stepped over to the closet and grabbed the first thing my hands landed on, a pair of black jeans. After wiggling into the near skin-tight pants, that described almost every pair I owned I tugged on a baby blue tank top, something I owned at least a hundred of in various colors and patterns, a pair of socks and some pale blue converse sneakers. I topped off the ensemble with a black denim jacket that mostly matched the jeans, kind of, but was much too thin to be of any help against the Montana winter, not that I cared.

I slipped down the stairs and out the front door as silently as I possibly could, actually managing to sneak past both of the parentals and all four ridiculous older brothers without being noticed. Only five more months and I could stop the sneaking around for fear of the third degree, my eighteenth birthday really couldn't come fast enough. Getting out of the house scot-free was a rare thing and when I realized roughly ten seconds later that I had actually managed to walk out without the car keys I rolled my eyes and just kept walking. There was no way in hell I was going back in that looney bin to get them and risking the onslaught of those nutcases, or rather my family, just for those damn keys. Instead, I tugged my cell phone out of my pocket as I reached the corner, unlocked the screen and hit speed dial number two, my best friend Abbey. I stood there, phone to my ear and what felt like a rather impatient look on my face, right foot tapping slightly to Abbey's ringback tone as I waited for the other girl to answer her phone.

"'Sup?" The short yet somehow very happy syllable from my best friend made me smile and shake my head a little, the girl was always in such a good mood.

"Hey, Abs. Can you pick me up?"

"Of course, girl. Where? And why don't you have your car?"

"The north-west corner and honestly, I managed to get out without being stopped this morning but…"

Abbey cut me off with a sharp giggle and I really could imagine the other girl shaking her head on the other end of the phone.

"But you walked out without your keys? Yeah, honey, with your family, I wouldn't go back for them either. I'll be there in five."

I, as usual, didn't bother to thank Abbey before we hung up, I would do that when the other girl showed up to relieve me from the chill of the morning air in a few minutes. The phone got shoved back into my pocket that really shouldn't have had space enough in it to allow such a thing and I took a slow, deep breath of the cool, clean, crisp morning air. It was a perfect morning as most of them were this time of year and the sun only just beginning to peek over the tree tops in the east made it that much better.

Exactly five minutes later, right on time as usual, Abbey pulled up and popped the door locks on her truck so I could hop in. I pulled the door shut and slipped on my seat-belt and then turned to grin at my best friend. Within seconds we were underway and Abbey was already on a roll about Tucker, the guy she'd been crushing on for the last couple years but had never had the guts to approach. I couldn't help myself, I just chuckled and shook my head a little, wondering for a moment how the perky and very attractive blond sitting beside me could possibly have any issue approaching anyone. Abbey was easily one of the best-looking girls in the pack and if she would just own that, well there was no doubt that she could have anyone she looked at. Abbey however seemed to have no clue how cute she was and despite my rather constant attempts at telling her over the years, the other girl just assumed that I was only being a good friend.

I quirked one slightly red and perfectly waxed eyebrow then took a few moments to study my best friend, something I did sometimes, just because I could do it and get away with it. Abbey was my height, five foot five, but we were built nothing alike, and didn't even look remotely alike for that matter. While I myself was rather solid, as least for my height, weighing in at about a hundred and forty-five pounds or so, Abbey rarely hit an even hundred and twenty. I was evenly built, well-proportioned and looked every bit the tomboy I had always been, meanwhile, the other girl was much more feminine, legs for miles. I normally kept my strawberry blond hair to about the mid-point of my shoulder blades and had it almost permanently in a ponytail. Abbey in contrast kept her naturally pale blond hair almost to her waist and very rarely pulled it up, letting it flow in soft curls over her shoulders.

Abbey had the more classically beautiful face, all smooth, clear skin, angled cheekbones and perfect lines with a light feathering of pale eyebrows and full lips. Meanwhile, mine had the softer 'Girl Next Door' look to it, a more rounded face, less defined features and more likely to be called 'cute' than 'stunning', 'beautiful', 'gorgeous' or even 'sexy'. All of those words had been used to define Abbey at some point or another during our friendship, some even slipping from my own mouth once or twice. Our eyes were the only place where we shared anything at all in common, we both sported pale but stunning ice blue eyes that grabbed, and often held, the attention of anyone that looked into them. I had to admit that I was perfectly fine with that being all we shared, while I had always known that I wasn't as gorgeous as my best friend, I knew that I wasn't exactly hard on the eyes either.

The sound of Abbey clearing her throat made me jump a little, thankfully just holding back the yelp that tried to escape but honestly not sure how long I'd had been lost in thought and staring at the other woman. How embarrassing. Abbey gave me an expectant look, both eyebrows raised, then nodded out the front window, indicating that we had stopped at the fork in the road that signaled the edge of the Clipper Packs territory and she needed to know where the hell she was going. We didn't have much planned now that I actually stopped and thought about it for a moment, we had just decided that we needed a day out away from the pack. It wasn't often that a wolf needed some alone time, we were social pack animals after all, but every now and then the human part of us won out and just needed a little space, and some silence. I sat there and glanced between the two forks for a moment, my face obviously showing that I was thinking far too hard about the choice.

Abbey made the decision for me after a moment by rolling her eyes and turning down the right fork, steering her truck toward the city. Most of the pack lived out in the farming area that we, the Clippers had called home for more than seven generations but a few that managed to pull off blending in with humans lived in nearby Billings. Abbey and I often went into the city for movies, shopping, dining and anything else we didn't have out in the middle of nowhere on the farms, which was pretty much everything. All I managed was to give a shrug and settle into my seat, knowing that if Abbey had decided on her own that she wanted to go into Billings, she had a reason for it and we would manage to find something to entertain us. Abbey turned on the radio and tuned it to the only station that came in properly so far out, a single country station which was fine by both of us strangely enough. We spent the rest of the drive into the city with the windows rolled down, the stereo cranked up and singing along at the tops of our lungs, badly.

CHAPTER TWO

BILLINGS OFFERED a few things that our small farming town just couldn't, besides the shopping and entertainment, it allowed those of us that weren't farmers or generational business owners to find jobs. Most of the pack lived by running 'from home' type businesses that had been in their families for generations. We had farmers, furniture makers, tailors and even a blacksmith that frequently made replicas for local renaissance events. In recent years, nurses, doctors, web designers and photographers had joined the ranks, adding more income to the pack. Each Alpha set up their pack differently when it came to keeping things running, in ours those that lived on pack land typically lived in homes that had been paid off for decades so they paid 'pack dues'. This money was held in a treasury that was handled by the Beta pair, it allowed the Alpha to lend a hand to those in need of financial assistance. It had worked for us for longer than most of the current pack had even been alive, so the practice stood. As teens in high school, Abbey and I were expected to hold down part time jobs, work ethics were important to the pack. Abbey worked in the general store in town that was owned by another family while I worked two hours after school most days in the local diner washing dishes.

It worked out for us and gave us some extra spending money so we could take these trips into town and get away for a bit. While being around our own kind was the way most of us preferred to live, getting out around normal humans was nice sometimes. We were only just reaching the point that the human world knew about us and most of the information leaking out was just rumors and speculation. Most packs were on the fence, but in the United States where our lands where there was a movement to get us out into the human world more, make friends, and work side by side. Those that advocated for the outing of our species believed that living and working beside the humans would make them more likely to accept us when our existence came to light. I fully believed that we should let the world know we were here, but had my doubts about the U.S. being the place to start that. As open as the country claimed to be there was a lot of hatred that could, and would be thrown our way, but the choice was rarely that of our generation.

My mind was on that line of thinking as we sang and drove and I was glad that I knew all of the songs by heart, it kept Abbey from catching that I was deep in thought. I wondered how long those old family businesses would last once the world knew about us and I wondered how long those of our kind would remain doctors, nurses and the like. We weren't human, not by any stretch, and most of us in the last two or three generations weren't even born as such. There was a time when our species was comprised almost completely of individuals that had been scratched or bitten. That was no longer the case these days as most packs, ours included had laws against attacking humans. Abbey and I and our parents were born werewolves, there were only a handful of members in the pack that bore scars from attacks but they were older and well-settled. The fact was that it was still a blood born disease and could be passed through a bite or scratch. We had been careful in recent decades, but that wouldn't stop the panic that I knew would follow if we were out in the open.

Then again, sometimes humans could shock us and that was what I had to hope for in this situation.

After a day of shopping and goofing off in a brand new arcade we happened across completely by accident, the two of us headed back toward home. The sun was just beginning to dip lower in the sky and we knew that dinner would be waiting for us when we finally made it back. We spent the drive back into pack territory chatting about that day's shopping trip and the games that we had played that afternoon at the arcade, each liking our own types. We were always in great moods after a day out together and even as the wind picked up and the clouds rolled in, our smiles didn't fade. The promise of a winter storm actually had both of us buzzing excitedly, our wolves shivering in anticipation of getting to run through fresh snow the next day. The animals could be a little silly and childlike about snow. That would be perfectly fine by us both since we each considered winter the favored of all the seasons.

By the time we arrived back at my house a light, feathery snow had started to fall and was already beginning to cling to the bed of Abbey's truck. We chatted and laughed as we slid out of the truck and made our way into the house, met immediately by my parents and a rather familiar-looking man seated in the living room. As the stranger turned to face us, he smiled and my brain kicked in as I realized that he wasn't such a stranger after all, though what the hell he was doing in my living room, well, I really had no idea. I glanced over to Abbey, unable, not to mention a bit unwilling, to return the man's smile, and then looked back to him before I shot quick looks to each of my parents. It was my father who spoke up after a few moments of extremely awkward silence.

"Abbey, you should probably head home, we have some family business to attend to. Kyndle, come in and sit down, we need to talk..."

Those four words had to be the most hateful things that I had ever heard come out of my father's mouth, or anyone's mouth in that moment thanks to the way he looked when he said them. 'We need to talk...' he might as well have said 'Let's go visit a firing squad' with the expression he was wearing. Tension gripped my body tightly and it was with every sense and nerve on high alert that I finally moved to the chair across from my father and sat down. Despite the way the cushions on the well-worn piece of furniture conformed to my body trying to relax me, something I normally loved about the thing, I stayed tense and on edge, sitting on the edge of the seat, ready to take flight if needed.

"Hey, relax." The voice came from slightly to my right and was followed by a hand being placed on my knee, an action which immediately ripped a growl from my throat, I did not like being touched.

Cameron, the man that had been sitting in the living room with my parents when I entered the house; chuckled a little and removed his hand from my knee, putting his hands up in front of him in a gesture of peace. So while unwelcome, he wasn't completely stupid, that was good to know, but I still wasn't happy with him or this situation. I relaxed just a fraction the moment his hand was off of me but a deep, low growl coming from my father made me turn my attention toward him. The glare that the man was leveling at me wasn't friendly in the slightest, not that he had ever really been the caring, friendly type, but the gaze still made my blood chill slightly in my veins then run a tad cold. I felt a small shiver ripple through me which, thankfully, no one else seemed to notice, and then I managed to force myself to look away from the harsh glare in my father's deep, charcoal eyes.

It took a moment to compose myself again before I looked up toward my mother, the older woman just sitting there, silently staring at her hands where they were folded in her lap. I knew that the woman wouldn't be any help at all since she had never really been one to stand up against her husband, no matter how nasty he got with me - his only daughter - but I would hope anyway. I let out a sigh, finally feeling like I wanted to know what the hell was going on in my house and why this other male was sitting in my living room.

"Okay, fine, I'm calm now, so what's going on?"

I stared at my father expectantly, hoping that he would just cut to the chase, not something that I thought was terribly likely, but again, I could hope.

"Kyndle, Cameron here came to us with a rather interesting situation, and an even more interesting possibility for a solution."

Yep, no chance for cutting to the chase, I could already feel an intensely long and very drawn out explanation coming on from the older male.

"This territory has belonged to the Clipper pack for generations, that much you already knew."

I nodded a little, already preparing for the boring expanse of pack history that I was sure was about to be driven my way and that, chances were, I already knew backwards and forwards. I was a damned Alpha after all.

"Well, what most don't know is that we bought the original tract of land in the southern section of the territory from the Rider pack, Cameron's pack."

I nodded again, even though I actually hadn't known that little bit of information, it really wasn't anything earth shattering or exciting, just a little piece of history. I was having difficulty understanding why I was getting this lesson on the territory and why Cameron needed to be present for it.

"The agreement between the packs was that, in exchange for that slip of land, the Clipper pack would help out the Rider pack if an issue ever arose that we could be of any assistance with. For the last few generations, nothing serious has come up and the little things that did emerge were either situations that we couldn't help with or were too small to need outside help. While we hadn't been needed, we continued to pass the reminder of that promise down from Alpha to Alpha, knowing that eventually, the time would come that we would be needed."

I leaned forward a little, my right elbow propped on my right knee and my chin rested on the heel of my hand as I held back a huff and forced back a roll of my eyes, not easy since those two things were about all I wanted to do just then. I was still completely lost on why the hell this conversation was happening and I just wanted him to get on with it and have it be over and done with.

"The thing is, if I may Dane." Cameron had spoken up beside me and I managed to glance over at him as my father did the same, I caught the older man's nod out of the corner of my eye. "Thank you. The thing is, Kyndle, my pack has hit some hard times the last generation or two and we could use a little help. We were hoping that things would work themselves out without our having to ask the Clippers to intervene for us, but, that just hasn't happened and we've hit a wall."

Now I was really confused and that, over everything else, actually made me straighten up a little and pay a bit more attention.

"The fact is this, the Riders are in serious trouble, the kind that we can't handle on our own."

I really had no idea what he was talking about; the Riders had never been anything but a big, strong, healthy pack so this seemed, well, unbelievable.

"Cameron, you aren't making any sense at all right now. The Rider pack is the biggest, healthiest pack in the country, probably on the whole damn continent. What the hell could possibly be happening that you couldn't handle on your own?"

The whole thing was making less and less sense the longer they talked and I really just wanted someone, anyone, to get to the damn point so I could leave this madhouse again.

"Besides, even if you need the packs help, why would we need to have this very weird and last-minute talk and why does it become a 'family' matter as my father obviously thinks it is. I mean, shouldn't this be a discussion happening between the packs as a whole? You know, rather than just the four of us in this room?"

That was bothering me more than almost anything else; it had been since I had settled myself into this damn chair. Why would something as big as helping out another pack not be discussed with everyone, each and every person in the pack should have a say in the matter and I didn't like that they weren't being given the chance to weigh in on the whole matter.

"The thing is, Kyndle... Well, this situation really isn't one that the whole pack needs to help out with, just the people in this room. To be honest, the Riders are in trouble, the kind that we can't get out of without help, your help. The pack is big but, well, we've run into a bit of a problem that we've never had to deal with before. Our members are leaned strongly into one age group or another right now, the over forty crowd and the rowdy preteens and teens. Most of the pack members my age are males and, well, frankly, a lot of the teens are male as well. We hit a rut of male pups being born into the pack the last couple decades and we're in danger, of losing our breeding opportunities. Without having a decent number of females within the pack to take as mates, our bloodline ends and the pack will die out."

"We considered merging with another pack but, at this point, all the surrounding packs are too large and well established to take in and actually have space for us. That said; we've decided, I've decided, that the best course of action for the moment is for me, as Alpha, to find a mate from outside the pack. It's a small step and in the long term it won't make much difference but, well, we figure that if we can get at least one new female in, maybe others will follow. It's the only option that seems to make any real sense and seems like it might actually work, so, after discussing it with your father, we came to an agreement."

Oh shit, I so did not like where this conversation was suddenly going and I suddenly became very aware that every muscle in my body was tense, ready to bolt into action and help me flee at the drop of a hat.

"Please tell me you aren't saying what I think you're saying."

I glanced at my father for any hint that those suspicions niggling at the back of my brain were just paranoia, but all I saw there was his usual hard, steady gaze and I knew that I was right. Dammit. I scanned the rest of the older man, honestly just trying to give myself a minute to process what the hell was happening. His cold, almost steel-colored eyes, at least they were steel -colored now that he wasn't pissed off at me, were set into a face that showed every one of its years in the lines set into the rough, tanned skin. His hard, angled jaw and perfectly set cheekbones showed that, at one point in his life, he must have been a rather attractive man. Anger had marred the features with deep furrows and the heavy signs of worry and his famous temper. A sweep of dark blond hair, shaggy from being ignored for months on end, had fallen across his forehead, threatening to cover his eyes if he let it get much longer.

I finished my assessment of my father and then realized that it hadn't really helped. I started to panic. My pulse was pounding in my ears and the rush of blood was almost too loud, making my head hurt. I needed out, away from what I was hearing, what they were planning and what I was about to be forced into doing if I understood right, and I was fairly damn certain I understood perfectly.

"I... I can't... Can't be here... I have to go..."

I made a move to stand up but before I could even get my ass up off the cushion a hand caught me by the arm and I turned on its owner with a snarl, my eyes meeting Cameron's and narrowing into a heated glare.

"Let go of me... Now"

"Kyndle, I know this is a lot to take in but, try to be reasonable here. My pack is in serious danger and, frankly, this is the only way I can see to help even a little."

"Well tough, I won't do it. Find another way."

"Kyndle..." My father's voice grabbed my attention and made me turn to look at him, his gaze serious and unwavering as I glared right at him.

"It wasn't a request, you're seventeen and while you are of bonding age, you are still under my law as your Alpha. I've given Cameron permission to take you as his mate and you **will** obey me. It isn't up for debate and you will do it or face the consequences. Am I understood?"

The glare fell off my face and was replaced by a look that I was sure mirrored the panic I had been feeling a few moments earlier. I honestly still couldn't believe what I was hearing and had to give my head a shake, let my eyes refocus and then look between the two men in my living room again. The looks on their faces confirmed that I wasn't dreaming, and that my world had just come crashing down around me.

"Kyndle? Have I made myself clear?"

"Yes."

"Good. The Bonding Ceremony will take place next Thursday."

CHAPTER THREE

THE WORLD fell away around me as I let the words sink in. Next Thursday, it was Friday, a week and my life as I knew it would be over, sentenced to spend the rest of my life with someone I was being forced to pair with. Someone I barely knew and, for what I did know of him, didn't even like. I managed to stay on my feet, hoping that I wasn't showing what I was feeling on my face. Everything in me was screaming at me to run away, put as much distance between myself and the men as I could. It was everything I could do to muster up the willpower to maintain my composure and get out a sentence, I just hoped my voice would stay steady.

"Fine, can I please just go and see Abbey now? We promised her mother I'd come over for dinner tonight."

I was desperate to get the hell out of my own living room and away from Cameron, who I realized at that moment still had a hand on my arm, something that I didn't like one bit. I watched as my father nodded and then yanked my arm away from Cameron's grasp, a bit more forcefully than was strictly necessary, and then was up from the chair and out the door before anyone could change their minds. I grabbed my keys and bolted out the door, slamming it behind me as I went. I made way down to my car and then tore out of the driveway and towards Abbey's house. I pulled into the driveway, slammed the car into park and then practically ran to my best friends' front door. If ever I had needed to see her, it was right this second, I was about to fall completely to pieces and that wasn't something I did. Ever.

I burst through the door, having given up on knocking before entering the place when Abbey and I were around eight years old. I shut the door as silently as I could and leaned back against it as it clicked shut. I let my head hang. My chin rested on my chest as a single tear slipped down my cheek. I really hated crying and I rarely did it so of course, it was just my luck that Abbey walked in just at that moment, apparently having heard me come in.

With my head down I couldn't actually see her, but I'd heard her footsteps and the scent of her cherry blossom perfume got stronger the moment we were in the same room together. For a moment she was silent and I could almost feel her eyes on me, trying to figure out why I was just standing there at her door the way I was. I knew how her brain worked and it was likely she was trying to decide how worried to be about me. Of course I picked that moment to sniffle despite my best efforts to not give away that I was crying. I could almost feel my best friend go tense at the sound, but when she spoke, she managed to keep from sounding overly worried.

"Kyndle...?"

I didn't respond, I couldn't actually put words together until I'd gotten my racing thoughts under control. To her credit, it seemed like she did her best to just let me get it together and answer her, but I took long enough that she stepped a little closer, her hand falling lightly on my shoulder.

"Kyn, talk to me. What's wrong?"

For a few more long seconds all I could was shake my head, not even sure I could make it through telling her what had happened without falling apart completely. I hated getting this emotional, though that was something that had been drilled into me from a young age by my father. An Alpha doesn't show weakness, physical or emotional, never let them see you cry, see you break. In a sudden and very pronounced urge to do every single thing he had ever told me not to, I let the walls drop. The dam broke and I sank to the floor with a sob, my head falling into my hands as Abbey dropped down beside me and wrapped me in a hug.

We sat like that for several minutes, but the tears finally ebbed and I took in a shuddering breath before I wiped my cheeks and heaved out a sigh. I knew I had to be a mess and I didn't much care, needing to tell her everything that had happened while I felt like I had the ability to get through it all without falling to pieces again.

I ran my fingers through my hair, eyes squeezed shut tight against another wave of tears threatening to break loose. Just the thought of repeating it all, and then actually having to see it through made me shiver. I wanted to wake up from this nightmare, get back to the life that I'd been living, the one where I wasn't being forced into this ridiculous pairing. That wasn't reality though, and this wasn't a nightmare, it was happening. If I had any chance of dealing with it, I would need Abbey's help and that meant telling her everything.

I rolled my shoulders, slammed my emotional walls back into place and swallowed hard before I tried to speak. Somehow, when I did finally open my mouth, while my voice was rough from crying for the last few minutes, the words came out steadier than I had expected.

"I need your help Abbey, I think my life just imploded around me..."

I still had my head down but I could hear Abbey moving to grab her coat seconds before the other girl moved me from in front of the door and pulled it open, shouting over her shoulder to her mother that she would be back in a bit. I felt Abbey's hand close around my wrist and finally looked up as my best friend pulled me to my feet and out the front door of the house. Her grip didn't ease up until we were down the driveway and on the sidewalk.

"Okay, talk."

My initial reaction was to take a ragged breath and shake my head as another tear managed to break free and slide down my cheek. I exhaled hard, a small growl escaping at the end at the little slip of emotion again. I clamped down harder on those barriers, I could break down later, right now I needed to tell her what happened and get some advice, or at least her opinion. I nodded, more to myself than her and forced myself to talk. What I didn't expect was to start rambling excessively but once I opened my mouth, the words tumbled without any real direction to them, so much for getting right to the point.

"My dad is completely insane if he thinks I'm actually following through with this shit. I mean, come on, what does he think I am? Does he think I'm his property? That he can just order me around? Does he think he can just go and sell me off to the highest bidder just because of some misplaced, generations old sense of responsibility?"

I had done what was habit to me, gone from crushed to totally pissed off in a matter of seconds and the cheeks that had been streaked by tears a few moments earlier were now flushed red with heated anger. I'd seen myself angry in mirrors often enough to know that my eyes would be flashing with that same anger. When I got like this the tended to flicker red around the edges of my irises and I'm sure I looked as if I was ready to kill someone right then and there. I wasn't far from it if I was being honest, just the memory of Cameron's face definitely left me thinking about it.

"Kyndle... What the hell are you..."

"Seriously, like, what does he expect me to do? No, I know exactly what he expects me to do. He expects me to be a good little girl, roll over and just do whatever my big, bad alpha tells me to do. God... It's like he thinks he literally owns me! Like he can just hand me over to whoever he wants whenever he feels like it! He's my father for crying out loud, not my slave master, and I don't like being treated like a damn piece of meat! Seriously, what the hell is this, the damn dark ages? I really think that he's lost his damn mind, he must have if he thinks I'm giving into this without a fight. Hell, I don't even like the guy and now he expects me to be mated to him for life?! No, not happening, not as long as I'm breathing and can kick them both in the damn balls, nope."

I realized too late that I didn't even let Abbey finish her question before I cut her off and started again. I hadn't even really heard her, just kept right on barreling forward with my rant, needing it out, exposed. I felt Abbey's hand on my shoulder again and despite the fact that I was so full of irritated energy I could probably run to Wyoming and back, at some point during my rant we had stopped walking. My hands were clenched into fists at my sides, my short-cropped nails digging into my palms. The sweet, stinging ripple I felt across the sensitive flesh meant I had probably broken the skin and that actually made me feel better for a moment.

I relaxed a fraction and turned to look at my friend, the tears starting to flow once more, this time in exasperation and anger rather than pain. I felt the rage ease away, replaced by a strange mixture of fear, panic and pain and I sniffed and attempted to get myself back under control. Abbey gave me a small, sympathetic smile as if she had picked up something of use from the ranting that had just been let loose in her general direction.

"So, what exactly happened? What has you so... Intense?"

All I could do was shake my head again, something I seemed to be doing a lot of today, and look down at my shoes for a few moments before I finally returned my gaze up to my friend and tried to explain in a calmer manner.

"Remember when we got to my house and my father said we had family business to attend to?" I glanced over at Abbey and waited for her to nod before I took a deep breath and continued on with my explanation. "Well, that guy that was in the living room with them, that was Cameron Kendall, the alpha of the Rider pack, you remember him."

"Yeah, I remember him, so I guess that's what the rant was about... I take it he's is making you do something you hate that involves Cameron?"

"He's forcing me into a bonding ceremony with him."

"Ewww! He's forcing a mate on you that don't want? Why?"

I gave her the short version of what the two men had told me and watched as her expression moved further and further into shock. Hell, I knew the feeling.

"That's... Well that's just insanity! I mean, I get wanting new blood in, but come on. Thinking that other women will follow because your father forced you into this is just nuts! What woman would want that? I mean, what female in their right mind would agree to be in a pack that forces bondings and matings?"

"Right? I'm wondering the same thing myself to be honest."

"Well, at least he's a good-looking guy. As shitty as this is, you can't exactly say no, Dane would, god who knows what he would do if you refused."

CHAPTER FOUR

I WENT rigid for a moment at my friend's words, my chest tightening, my stomach knotting and every muscle in my body itching to lash out at the comments. I forced myself to calm down enough to look over at her, my brows furrowed as I studied her for several beats. I was trying to decide if I'd heard her right and if so, if she had actually meant the words or if she was being snarky. Sometimes it was hard to tell with her and I didn't want to blow up at her for a badly timed joke.

"Wait... You're saying that you think I'm agreeing to this madness?"

"Well, Kyndle, do you really have a choice? You know that if you say no he'll probably just kick you out on your own. You're one tough bitch honey, but I don't think you have it in you to be a lone wolf."

No, we don't have that in us at all...

My wolf was whimpering at me from the back of my mind and I knew deep down that she was right, as tough and independent as I liked to think that I was, tried to pretend I was, I was no loner and I knew it all too well.

"You're right, I don't have that in me at all, I wouldn't survive it. So I guess I have no choice..."

I wasn't happy about that in the slightest, honestly wishing that I had a way out that didn't involve being mated to Cameron. Abbey was right, he wasn't a bad looking guy, and at least he was an alpha, just like me. Or rather, like I should be if my father would stop being such an alpha male about the whole thing. That knowledge didn't make the situation any easier to stomach. I sighed heavily and sat down hard on the curb, my elbows on my knees and my head hanging down as I shook it.

I was in some serious trouble and I knew it, I was torn and broken inside. I knew that there was nothing I could really do about the situation, but I still had hope that I might find some way out. Cameron wasn't terrible. On second thought, maybe he was. The fact was that I didn't really know the man at all outside the few times we had met when I was younger, before he had taken over his pack. I'd met their previous alpha and while he was a strong and confident man, he had a god complex and I'd always thought that he needed to be knocked down a peg or two.

If Cameron was following in his footsteps, well, we were definitely going to have issues, me and my new mate. I understood that as an alpha male he was bound to be a bit of an ass, it was something that tended to plague the dominant males of the species, but that didn't mean I had to take it sitting down. No, I would damn well make sure that he knew that he'd met his match in me if I was about to be forced to be with him for the rest of my life. I wouldn't lay down and take being walked all over and controlled like my mother had. Like so many other females who should be powerful in their own right.

No matter what I had to do, that would not be me. Then again, that entire topic in itself brought up its own issues, very painful issues that made it hard for me to breathe. The tears prickled at the corners of my eyes again just thinking about them and I was having to fight harder and harder to keep them at bay.

"There's only one problem with that, Abbey..."

"What's that? That you don't really know him?"

"I could get over that... But I'm in love with someone else."

That made Abbey cock her head a little toward me and raise an eyebrow, waiting for me to elaborate and when I didn't, she asked, just like I knew she would.

"Who?"

"No one you know. Actually, someone else from the Rider pack."

When I glanced over again, my comment had caused both her eyebrows to arc high on her forehead and her eyes to widen significantly since Cameron was the only Alpha male in the Rider pack. It was well known in our world that an Alpha female developing feelings for a wolf lower than another Alpha was almost completely unheard of.

"Seriously? How do you know you're in love?"

"Well, for one it's been going on for two years. And I don't really know exactly how to explain it but... She knows." I held my hand over the center of my chest, indicating that I was talking about the wolf and my friend nodded, understanding coloring her features. "Trust me, Abbey, it's definitely love. And I think if I have to be mated to Cameron I'd rather just die."

That made Abbey slide over and put an arm around my shoulders and while it made me feel quite a bit better, I had to wonder if she would stay where she was if she knew the revelation I was about to lay on her.

"Well damn girl. Two years. I guess that's long enough to know that the person and the wolf are on the same page. It's just so... Well, weird."

"Why is it weird?" I was speaking with my head on her shoulder at this point, taking in all the contact I could while I had the chance to do so.

"I've just never heard of an Alpha having any kind of bond, emotional or otherwise, with anything other than another Alpha."

"It is another Alpha, Abbey."

I glanced up and saw her looking down at me, the confusion written all over her face as she tried to understand what I was saying, Cameron didn't have any brothers.

"How?"

"It's Frost. Cameron's younger sister."

My eyes had settled back on the pavement as I practically whispered the words. I had just outed myself to my best friend, something I probably should have done years earlier, but had never managed. I felt her tense a little beside me and I waited, holding my breath, afraid to move or even breathe. For her shift away from me like I expected. She didn't and every second that ticked by I relaxed a fraction, allowing myself to hope that she was actually good with this.

"Well... Damn."

She sighed and reached over to wrap her other arm around me and gave me a tight squeeze before she kissed the top of my head. That did it, my best friend had apparently accepted who and what I was and that was all it took to open the floodgates, again. I turned into her, wrapped my arms around her waist, buried my face in her shoulder and cried. She let me, holding me closer and rocking me slightly, letting me get it all out and not trying to stop me or attempting to talk until the tears died down a few minutes later.

"Okay, sit up, we need to talk."

I nodded and sat up, wiping my eyes and she pulled a tissue out of her pocket and handed it to me so I could blow my nose. That done I took a deep breath and let my eyes meet hers, seeing concern, understanding, support and love there. She smiled at me and I actually smiled back a little bit, which felt good but didn't dull the piercing ache that had been rapidly forming in my heart.

"I just don't know what to do Abbey. I can't spend the rest of my life with him. My heart already belongs to Frost."

And so does mine...

Yeah, I knew that, my wolf loved the free-spirited girl as much as I did and I knew she and her wolf felt the same, we'd had this discussion months ago.

"Why don't you just tell your dad? About Frost I mean... Seriously, he might be okay with it, she's still technically an Alpha even though she's not pack leader."

"I can't... I already know how he would react."

"And how's that?"

"He'd mate me off to Cameron right then and there. No chance to think, no second guesses, done."

Abbey just shook her head, almost like she couldn't believe that my father would do something so drastic, the rest of the pack didn't know him like I did.

"He would Abbey. Because the only other alternative wouldn't be as easy, or as profitable, for him."

"And what's the other option?"

"Run me out of the pack, out of the territory, banish me."

"Just for falling for a girl? He wouldn't."

"He already has... Remember Diana and Grier?"

"Of course, they left, what, like five years ago? Joined other packs."

"No Abbey, they didn't leave or join other packs. He caught them together and he lost it. He said that he wouldn't have that kind of sickness in his pack. Two females together can't produce pups and therefor doesn't further the pack so it's wrong. He gave them a choice, bond with males in the pack, or leave. They chose each other and he banished them, permanently."

I heard Abbey gasp beside me and knew that she hadn't been expecting that at all, no one in the pack would. He was, after all, their all-knowing, understanding and caring leader and he only wanted what was best for all, what made the pack happy. Yeah, sure he did, as long as it was exactly what was best for him and conformed to his view of the world.

"Well shit."

Yeah, that just about summed it up in one word and as Abbey looked back out over the field across the street she let out a heavy sigh and one of my own followed it.

"Well we have to come up with something, Kyndle. We've both watched and seen what happens when an emotional bond forms with one wolf but a physical bond is forced with another."

All I could do was nod to that since we hated talking about it, the whole process. All wolves did. It could take years to happen but the physical bonding without the emotional bond as support, without the love, it wore both parties down but always seemed to affect the female much worse than the male. First would be a depression, the loss of that spark that made us what we are, that made us so vibrant and so alive. Then anger settled in, a deep seated, dark anger that ate away at the soul and left our human side violent and quick tempered. The wolf went mad inside us, driving us to hurt those around us.

"Trust me Abbey, I know. I've been watching it happen since the day I was old enough to pay attention to what the hell was happening in my house."

Abbey's gaze snapped to me, slightly confused and then she seemed to grasp what I had just told her and she hugged me again. My mother had been forced into the pairing with my father, given to him so that he would take in her smaller pack and make them members of the Clipper pack. She was in the third stage, grief, loss, emotional devastation. The wolf had simply given up trying to fight for what it wanted, had laid down, rolled over and refused to bother any further with the human that apparently hated it enough to ignore it. The spark was dead, long gone, and my mother no longer had it in her to disagree with my father. Meanwhile, he was still in stage two, had been since I was about three and almost constantly as angry as a badger with its tail caught in a bear trap.

"I didn't know. I'm so sorry."

I just shrugged; how could she know? No one knew, my mother wasn't ever allowed to leave the house so nobody ever saw how flat and dead her eyes were and when he wasn't at home raging at me, my father was the perfect Alpha. I couldn't really remember when exactly I had started hating my parents, but the feeling hit me full force just then. A raw hatred for a man who would force me into something that I didn't want and that would end up killing my spirit, my very soul. Definitely for my mother, a woman who knew exactly how it felt to have her heart ignored, to feel as if it were being ripped from her and smothered and sat back, said and did nothing, allowing him to do the same to me.

Chapter Five

We sat there in silence for a few minutes, just staring across the fields and watching the snow continue to fall lightly. "So let's fight this."

"I don't know how, Abbey."

"There has to be a pack somewhere that would respect what the two of you have and take you in. We just need to find one of them and the two of you can run away together."

"Think you can find one of those packs in a week?" She looked at me shocked and I just pursed my lips and little and nodded that she had heard me right.

"A week? Seriously?"

"Yep. Next Thursday. Kinda sucks, I haven't even had the chance to see her the last few weeks. Now I may have to stand there as her brother's new mate the next time I do see her." Pain rippled through me and the wolf whined beneath the surface, the sound echoed from my human form. "I hate this."

"I hate this for you." She let out a soft sigh and then I felt her suck in a deep breath and sit up a little straighter. "No, we're gonna figure this out. Let's go inside. You can write her a letter, tell her what's going on and I'll run it over there, my movements won't be watched like yours are. If you just go home and let me handle it then it should be okay."

I didn't think that writing her a letter would make any difference but all I could do was nod, at least she was trying to help. We stood and brushed ourselves off then made our way into her house and up to her room where I sat down to work on this letter. I started and stopped several times, not really knowing what to say or, if I had an idea of what, not knowing how. After some help from Abbey, I managed to get something I thought would work, signed it and then stuffed it into an envelope and handed it to Abbey. She took it with a nod and then without a word we headed downstairs, loaded up into our respective vehicles and I headed home.

I stepped through the front door and heard the vague sound of a male voice calling my name from somewhere to my left. I ignored it and made my way upstairs, my eyes on my shoes the entire time. My father's voice barely creaked through into the haze of heartache weighing me down. Somewhere, deep down, I had known that my days with Frost were limited and that we would be torn apart eventually. I guess I just figured that I'd have a little more time with her, more than what we'd had up to now and it hurt that I would be losing her already.

I eased the bedroom door closed behind me, locked it and shuffled to my bed, not even bothering to turn a light on even though it was pitch black in my room. My night vision was as good as any other of my species and I could see just fine with the sliver of moonlight filtering in between the curtains. I kicked off my shoes, dropped my jacket to the floor and collapsed onto my bed, curling up into a ball clutching one of my pillows as I cried yet again, this time alone and silently. Everything that mattered to me, the one person I loved more than anything in the world, was being ripped away from me and there wasn't a damn thing I could do to stop it from happening.

Eventually I drifted off into a fitful and dreamless sleep, still clutching the pillow, the one under my head soaked in tears and visions of the pale blonde that had been the center of my world for the last two years flitting through my mind. They came and went as if carried by some unseen breeze, flickering in to tease me, to show me what I'd had right there in my life. As if laughing at me, telling me that I could no longer have it, no longer have her and even as I slipped in and out of sleep, my heart hurt.

Frost had taken my breath away the moment I laid eyes on her for the first time when I was eleven and it had been that instant that I realized I wasn't like my other female friends. While the Clipper and Rider packs lived on two separate patches of land, all the underage wolves attended the same schools, at least, the ones who attended public schools. Frost was the same age as Abbey and I and had started at our school in the sixth grade. She was in my homeroom class that year and when she walked in that first day, I missed an entire two minutes of what Abbey had been saying to me just watching her walk across the room and find her seat.

Her hair was naturally that shade of blonde that people attempt by bleaching but never manage, shone like spun silk and was cropped just at the tops of her shoulders. She somehow managed to be even more pale than I was, a feat to say the least. Her eyebrows, matching her hair in color, sat in perfectly shaped arches above what had to be the most stunning eyes I had ever seen on anyone. They were a slightly-paled violet that anyone could tell was definitely purple even from across the room.

I couldn't even begin to count the number of times over the last two years that I had gotten lost in those eyes and not cared one bit. She was stunning, perfect and even back then she made my stomach flutter, my throat close up a little and my brain go fuzzy. That reaction had yet to dull even the slightest fraction even after spending the last two years staring into them. She had leaned over to ask the person sitting next to her where one of the hallways was about halfway through homeroom and her voice left a smile on my face. Then she laughed, and I thought I was about to fall right out of my seat but caught myself, not that it was easy. She had one of those laughs that could cheer you up no matter how bad your day had been. It made me want to laugh along and made me feel like everything would be okay if she would just laugh one more time.

The sound of my wolf whining pathetically into my sleepy brain jolted me awake and what had been a sliver of moonlight through the curtains was now vibrant golden sun. I squinted at it for a moment and considered just staying in bed, then remembered that Abbey had taken a letter to Frost for me the night before. I bolted out of bed, stripped down, showered in record time and then dressed just as fast, still trying to get my left shoe on as I hopped toward the stairs. My keys were, thankfully, in my hand already and even though my entire family was seated at the dining table, and called me to join them, I didn't stop. I left the house, was in the car and out of the driveway by the time my father made it to the front door to call me back. I didn't stop, I couldn't, I had to see if Abbey had found her, if she'd gotten the letter, read it, if she'd said anything.

I ignored the speed limit and pulled into Abbey's driveway in half the time it would normally take me to get to her house. I was out of the car the moment it was in park, up the steps and through the door, shouting a quick good morning to her parents as they welcomed me. My best friend was still in bed when I barged into her room and I just jumped right in the middle of her bed. That jostled her awake and she grumbled and looked up at me, growling slightly then chuckling as I shook her and bounced on her bed. She glanced over at the clock and then back at me with a pout.

"You are far too excited for this hour... What do you want girl?"

"Pfft, like you don't know. What happened? She get the letter?"

Abbey yawned, stretched and then sat up and took her time rubbing her eyes and running her fingers through her hair. I was getting impatient and she damn well knew it, she was doing this on purpose and I hoped that meant she had some kind of news.

"Yes, she got the letter. Handed it to her myself."

"And?"

"And nothing. Cameron was home and he yelled at her to get back inside so she said she'd have to read it later and went back in the house. That's it."

That was it? Really? Well, at least she had the letter, that was something and while I would have felt better if Abbey could have waited while she read it and gotten a reply, I would take what I could get right now. I nodded a little, sighed and flopped myself down on the bed beside her to which her reaction was to roll her eyes, slide from the bed and head for the bathroom. I laid there and waited for her to come back, staring at the ceiling and just thinking, letting all the memories of the last two years filter through my mind.

I glanced over as Abbey hopped back into the bed and stretched out next to me, acting as if I hadn't just admitted that I liked girls to her yesterday. That was why she was my best friend, nothing I said or did seemed to faze her. I let out a little laugh and she looked over at me like I had lost my mind, one eyebrow quirked up as if to ask me 'what?'.

"Sorry girl, I was just thinking that you seem so completely oblivious and unfazed by all of this."

"All of what? You and Frost?" I nodded a little to that since she had it right on, not needing to say anything else, just watching her grin a little. "Kyndle, I don't really care who the hell you decide to get it on with. As long as you're happy, I'm happy."

"I know that, that was never my concern about telling you."

"Then what took you so long?"

"I was actually worried things might get weird between us. That you might think I was, like, flirting with you all the time or something."

"You do flirt with me all the time. And I flirt right back. It's our thing, what we do, no big deal."

"Touché. Alright... I was also worried about... Well..."

"The fact that Frost and I could be related, we look that much alike?"

"Yeah. That." She just laughed and shook her head at me as she looked over, stared at me for a few seconds and then leaned over close and put her forehead against mine.

"You worry too much. Look, honey, I know that this is a huge deal for you, coming out and all, but really, I couldn't care less. We've been best friends our whole lives. I loved you to pieces before you told me yesterday and you know what? I still love you just as much today." She moved to kiss my forehead then and lingered just a few seconds then leaned back, her hands still on my cheeks. "Okay?"

"Okay. And Abbey... Thanks." I smiled a little and she just smiled back and shot me a little playful wink that made me giggle a bit. "So, what are doing today? I am so not going home until I absolutely have to."

"Arcade?"

"Arcade!" With that she hopped up, got dressed and we loaded into my car and headed back into Billings for another date with some video games.

CHAPTER SIX

THE DAY had been a success and had managed to ease my growing tension, distract me and keep me out of the house until everyone fell asleep, just like I'd wanted. I slipped in and went right to bed, feeling a little better but still worried. I hadn't heard from Frost yet, not that we ever really called or texted, not with her brother getting her phone bill and my father getting mine. The last thing we needed was to be caught sending incriminating text messages so we just didn't. Deep down I hoped that I would see her at school the next day but since we didn't have any classes together, I would have to wait until lunch. We typically didn't interact much at school, terrified we'd get too distracted, get caught and then we'd be in real trouble. I managed to force myself into a terrible night of sleep that was plagued with those same fleeting images of the gorgeous blonde.

The next morning came and dragged me out of what I suppose qualified as sleep before I was really ready to be awake, but I forced myself out of bed and into a warm shower. I picked clothes, still half asleep, dealt with my hair and brushed my teeth before I managed to practically lumber down the stairs like a zombie. I waved off breakfast, feigning an upset stomach that was actually just all tied in nervous knots and lugged my backpack to the car to head to school. I was almost three months into my senior year and had wanted it to be over for the last two months, no such luck. I trudged into school, feeling only slightly more awake than when I'd crawled out of bed and forced myself to sit still and pay attention through my first three classes.

I almost cheered when third period let out for lunch but that excitement was short lived as I sat in the cafeteria with Abbey looking for Frost, not seeing her. Fifteen minutes into lunch period, I turned to Abbey with a frown creasing my brow and huffed a little.

"She's not here. She never misses school, she's even more intent than me about attendance."

I was so confused and as I sat there and scanned the room one more time, a terrifying thought swarmed over me and made my skin chill and my heart seize a little.

"Abbey, what if she read my letter and... What if this is her answer? Not showing up for school, staying away from me?"

The grip on my heart tightened at the thought and I suddenly felt like the floor was falling away under me. My stomach suddenly felt the need to part ways with the portion of my lunch I'd managed to eat. I was out of my seat and to the door in seconds with Abbey on my heels all the way to the bathroom, which I barely made it into. Being the great best friend she was, she held my hair as what little I had managed to eat came back in a rather spectacular display. She sat there and rubbed my back as I was wracked by a series of dry heaves and then stayed as I cried again, at least the fourth time in three days, unheard of for me.

Once I was sure my stomach had settled I leaned back and she got up long enough to grab me a bottle of water from her backpack and some paper towels to wipe my face and blow my nose. I was a mess and I knew it, though I honestly couldn't be bothered to care at that moment in time. I felt terrible so looking it just fit.

"You okay?"

"I don't know Abs. I really don't."

She didn't say anything else, just sat there and hugged me one armed, knowing better than to start placating me with shit I didn't want to hear like 'it'll be okay' and 'it'll all work out'. All those cliché, chick flick bullshit things would only make it worse. The warning bell sounded for the beginning of fourth period and I looked over at her, silently asking if she needed to leave me there and get to class. She just shook her head, not saying a word, and pulled me over closer so I could lean my head on her shoulder. I really couldn't have asked for a better best friend right then and I honestly knew deep down that if it wasn't for her, I wouldn't be dealing with this even half as well as I was.

She sat there in silence with me all the way through fourth period and as the bell rang to let class out, I finally felt like I could get up and walk without crying, puking or passing out. I told Abbey as much and she helped me up, handed me my backpack and walked out of the bathroom with me.

"Hey?" I turned to look at her, standing just a few feet away from me now since our fifth period classes were in opposite directions. "No matter how tough this is, you're tougher and you'll get through it. I'm right here with you. No matter what."

"Thanks Abs. I love you, you know that?"

"Of course you do, I'm amazing."

We both smiled a little and she laughed at herself then seemed to let the seriousness take over her features a little one more time.

"And I love you too, Kyndle. Hang in there."

I nodded and managed another half-hearted smile then we both turned and walked toward our respective classes. Fifth period I had math, calculus to be exact and while I actually rather liked math, it was a quiz that I was neither prepared for or with it enough to focus. By the time the bell rang I knew I had failed the thing miserably which just sucked since it would be the first and my father might actually have to sign it if it was too bad. I hauled myself into my sixth and final class of the day, French IV and knew that if I had any chance at concentrating on anything today, this would be it. Apparently, even my love of the French language couldn't break my funk and the teacher asked me to hold back after class.

"Are you feeling okay today Miss Callahan? It seemed like you were somewhere else."

"Sorry. I'm dealing with some personal issues, it's been a rough weekend."

"Anything you want to talk about?"

I just shook my head, I wasn't ready to get into the details of my personal life with anyone other than Abbey at this point. Definitely not until I knew what was going on with Frost and why she had missed school and if it had anything to do with me, with us. She seemed to realize that I was done talking about it and dismissed me so I bolted for the senior parking lot as fast as I could. Abbey was standing beside my car when I got to it and, knowing the look I was sporting meant I was over talking about it, just hugged me. We stood there for a few minutes, not speaking, just her holding me and letting me try and get it together enough to drive.

Once I thought I'd be okay, I patted her shoulder and she let go and backed away, giving one of my hands a light squeeze before she headed for her truck to go home. I did the same, doing the best I could to ignore my family for the rest of the night. I claimed I had twice as much homework as I did so I could eat dinner alone in my room and finally gave up trying to do the homework I did have and attempted to sleep. That went about like it had the last two nights and it was beginning to wear on me, both mentally and emotionally as well as leaving me drained of my normal energy.

I was losing that spring in my step and it was wearing me down even further. I got what I could and then pulled a 'lather, rinse, repeat' of the day before, minus the lunchroom breakdown and visit with the toilet afterward. Still no Frost and I was beginning to feel like this was meant to be a statement, to tell me something and that I was stubbornly refusing to accept it as such. I'd said it out loud sure, but that was miles away from actually accepting it as the truth. However, the feeling only increased as I reached Thursday and still hadn't seen Frost, or heard from her, which scared me. I was losing it along with what little hope I had left that I could get out of this thing with Cameron.

She had abandoned me, left me to this fate that would leave me hollow and unhappy and I wanted to find her, shake her and scream at her. I wanted to know why and I couldn't even ask her because she hadn't been at school all week, hadn't called, hadn't texted, hadn't written. Nothing. I had ridden to school with Abbey that morning because my parents, rather my *Alpha*, insisted that she should bring me to the ritual clearing instead of driving there myself.

I think he was expecting me to try and run. I'd definitely considered the thought early on, but well, where the hell would I run to now? And who for? I had nothing left, no reason to run, no one to run for and I had slipped into a deep depression somewhere around lunch that had wrapped what was left of my heart in ice. We pulled silently into the ritual clearing and Abbey parked, sitting there quietly and just staring out the windshield for a few minutes before she finally broke the silence.

"Maybe she couldn't get to you, ya know? Like, something happened and she didn't have the chance."

"Like what Abs? What would possibly keep her from school and keep her from calling, texting and writing?" I snapped at her when I spoke and immediately felt like a jerk for it, this wasn't Abbey's fault.

"I don't know Kyn, I'm just trying to help."

"I know Abs, I'm sorry. I'm just beyond caring at this point. I just wanna get this over with so I can settle into being depressed…"

I could feel the sympathy rolling off of her in waves, I could even smell it and had it been anyone else, I would have been pissed off, but coming from Abbey it was just what I expected. She cared about me and I knew she hated seeing me like this, so depressed that I'd given up completely. I shook my head, popped the door and slipped out of the truck, leaving the door open so Abbey could get our stuff from the seat behind mine. I wandered out into the clearing without paying much attention to where I was headed, just needing to walk and not think. I was vaguely aware that I had stopped after several yards but I was so out of my head and body at that point that it barely registered.

CHAPTER SEVEN

"HEY KYN." I had been leaning against a tree opposite the truck, daydreaming about Frost again despite my efforts to be pissed at her, but Abbey's voice yanked me back to reality.

"Yeah?"

"So... I may have a little good news." I just stood there, leaned back against the tree, arms crossed over my chest and waited for her to tell me what this news was. "I happened to run into your dad and, well, I started chatting with him about the bonding and I mentioned to him that you were quite a bit younger than his pack females usually mate. He agreed and said it was necessary and blah, blah, blah and I asked him why he makes them wait so long. He said he believes that our females should finish high school and at least think about starting college before being bonded." I just raised an eyebrow at her, not sure where she was headed with this whole thing but slightly curious if I was being honest.

"He said that it's good for our females to have a good head on their shoulders before they started a family. I asked him if he thought that you deserved less courtesy than his Omega females and he thought about it for a minute. I guess he got my point because he called Cameron over and told him that the final bonding was not allowed to take place until after you graduated high school in May."

"I appreciate that Abs, I really do. But it doesn't really change much. I mean, it really just means that I can keep him from touching me for another few months but doesn't stop what I'm being forced to do. You know the bond is three parts, mind, body and soul. The mind bonds here, tonight... in five months he'll take my body as well. Then, my soul will rebel against the bond and I'll lose myself to it."

It wasn't that I didn't appreciate her help, I did, more than she probably knew, but it didn't change things. I would be bonded to Cameron and I would be stuck with him forever, I could already feel my soul dying a little as my wolf whimpered, crying for her mate, for Frost. Abbey just nodded a little and hugged me, I hugged her back fiercely, making sure she knew how much I appreciated everything she had done for me the last few days. Then I attempted to silence the wolf within, her incessant whining and whimpering tearing my heart to pieces.

I walked with my best friend to the center of the clearing as the sun dipped below the horizon and stood in front of the man that I was about to be given to, forced into being with. Damn I hated him. My wolf hated him too. She didn't want him, didn't want him to touch us, wanted to rip his throat out and leave him bleeding in that clearing. She couldn't do that though, not without a reason and, to be honest, without some kind of conformation from Frost I had no reason, and neither did she.

The ceremony played out with Abbey looking almost as pained as I did standing there, knowing what this was doing to me, that helped a little, but not much. It was a quick thing, the bonding ceremony, and was typically followed by the new pair sealing the bond physically, but since my father had insisted I finish school first, I wouldn't have to deal with that particular stomach-turning event tonight. Instead, the elders of both packs, present for and involved in the ceremony, decided a midnight run was in order for the new 'Alpha Pair'. I cringed at the thought and sound of it, I didn't want to be in a 'pair' of any kind with Cameron, yet, here I was.

I watched as the others present shifted forms and instead of feeling the excitement that usually came with preparing for a run, I just wanted to break down and cry. Abbey padded her way up beside me, her light blonde wolf standing with her head just above my hip, those bright blue eyes piercing right through me. A tear slipped down my cheek as I ran my fingers through my best friends silky fur and she let out a happy little wolfish purr and nuzzled against me. With a deep breath, I turned, stripped out of my clothes and started to run, Abbey at my side.

Mid-leap over a log on the opposite side of the clearing, I shifted in the air, landing on four feet rather than two. I slid to a stop, Abbey doing the same on my left and Cameron on my right which prompted me to look over at him. His large, deep brown wolf stood at least three inches taller at the shoulder than mine, almost five inches taller than Abbeys. The dark chocolate fur gleamed under the moonlight and given better circumstances, he might have been attractive in both forms.

As it stood, I just couldn't do anything but want him as far away from me as possible and as he stepped closer I backed up beside Abbey, eyes narrowed at him. He took a couple steps closer and my own wolf, a stunning and rather unnatural pale ginger in color that damn near matched my hair, peeled her lips back, revealing massive canines, and growled a warning at the larger male. He hesitated just a moment and then glared back, huffed and bounded off into the woods which allowed me to relax a little. Abbey and I waited a few moments to make sure he was gone and then took off in the opposite direction together.

We ran for what seemed like days but turned out to actually only about three hours and then found ourselves back in the clearing. We shifted back and had almost finished putting our clothes back on when the rest of the party bounded in, shifted and started dressing.

"That was pretty tacky of you Kyndle, running off like that on our bonding night."

Cameron's voice, and his words, just made me roll my eyes without bothering to turn around and face him. It was disrespectful, highly so, and I couldn't have really cared any less just then. He could huff about it all he wanted.

"Kyndle." My father's voice was harsh and commanding and did actually succeed in making me turn to face the two males. "Your mate was speaking to you. Show him some respect and look at him when he addresses you, then speak back."

"Why?" This single word seemed to anger both males and I could actually see Cameron's hands clenching at his sides and his neck and ears turning red.

"Listen woman, you are my mate now and you will show me some respect. I demand it." He was right up in my face, invading my personal space and I was holding myself back from hitting him with everything I had in me.

"Demand all you want Cameron. My father said I had to bond to you, not that I had to respect you or even like you. Those things are earned and so far, neither of you have earned either. So unless you plan on beating me into submitting to you like he did to my mother, get the hell out of my face."

Now they were both fuming and I knew that I was likely in for a rough night regardless of where I spent it but I didn't care. I shoved past the fuming Alpha and then stepped around my father. At least I tried to, but he halted my progress with a hand, right across my cheek. I turned on him with a growl, blue eyes flashing red in the dark and had to fight to get myself under control.

"I hope that felt good. Hope it made you feel like the big bad Alpha male you try to be. I hate you both."

With that I turned and left the clearing, Abbey's truck starting up behind me and I knew she would meet me out at the road. Sure enough the truck was waiting for me when I exited the woods onto the road and I climbed into it and settled in for the ride home. We were silent for the first few minutes until my phone chimed that I had a text message so I pulled it from my pocket and flipped it open. It was from my father, telling me that I had better either come home or be at Cameron's tonight. I had the urge to tell him to fuck off and go to Abbey's but I knew that would just get her into trouble so I had her take me home.

She pulled up in front of the house and I gave her a quick hug then hopped out of the truck and made my way inside. I hadn't been prepared for more than my father but he wasn't alone when I stepped into the living room, Cameron stood beside him, arms crossed over his chest and looking a little too smug for my liking.

"Why's he here?"

"He's your mate Kyndle, like it or not. You're bonded now and he has every right to be here, and to take you home with him, which he wants to do."

"What? No... I don't think so. You said that the second stage had to wait until I graduated. I am not going to an empty house with him. Not happening."

The expression settled across my father's face told me that no matter how much I protested, I was going whether I wanted to or not, even if they had to carry me. Great, just what I needed. Well, I wasn't about to make it easy on them, that was for damn sure, I would fight this every step of the way, as hard as I could.

"No, I'm not leaving. Screw both of you."

I started to walk past them and Cameron reached out and grabbed hold of my left wrist as I tried to pass. I looked down to where he had a grip on me and growled then looked back up at him, anger flashing across my features. He just held on tighter.

"You're going. Period."

With that he picked me up and, thanks to the fact that he was almost six inches taller than me and outweighed me by at least seventy pounds, tossed me over his shoulder like I was a damn doll. I kicked and thrashed against him, trying to get him to put me down but he simply chuckled and walked to the door. He stepped outside, walked to the driveway and dropped me into the open passenger seat of his truck then slammed the door. I tried the handle but the bastard had flipped the child safety locks and it wouldn't open from the inside. He slid into the driver's seat, saluted my father and then started the truck up and pulled out, heading toward Rider territory and my new fate.

I was pissed and plotting my escape, not that there was much chance of getting away, he was just as fast and agile as I was and could track as well. I was so screwed. I was still fuming silently when we pulled to a stop and it took me a few moments to realize that we had actually pulled up to his house. Half of me had expected him to take me to some shady hotel halfway between the towns, but here we were. His house. The house he shared with Frost. She could be in there right now and just thinking about seeing her again made my chest tighten and my stomach flip nervously. He hopped out and came around the truck to open my door. He kept a vice-like hold on me as I got out then led me to the door and inside the house. Once he had the door locked up and knew I couldn't leave, he released the death grip on my wrist and I rubbed it a little.

"Look, you disrespected me today and I don't intend to let that slide. Besides, you have a few things to learn besides respect."

"Like what?"

"Like how this society works little girl."

"Little girl? What are you, like, six years older than me? Seven maybe?"

"Age is just a number, Kyndle. And I mean this..."

I rolled my eyes but then looked down at what it was he had just shoved at me and my heart stopped for a minute. It was the envelope, still sporting my practiced scripting, that I had sent Frost's letter in, that meant he had read it. My eyes snapped up to meet his and in a matter of seconds fear, anger, panic and sheer terror had to have flickered through my eyes. He had definitely seen it all. He smirked at me and took a few steps forward, forcing me to back up a couple steps but I hit the wall behind me and had to stop.

"I think you were hoping my baby sister would save you from me. But how, I have to wonder. What was she supposed to do, Kyndle? Hmmm? Rush in and declare her love in front of your dad and the elders? I don't think so. She knows her place and intends to take it, you were just a fling."

CHAPTER EIGHT

THE COLOR drained from the world, everything going fuzzy around the edges as the room seemed to close in on me. The ache in my heart spread until I felt like it was actually, literally breaking in half. I bit back a sob and tried to square my shoulders, though I wasn't feeling very confident about anything at the moment.

"You're lying." I said the words but even as they left my mouth, my voice cracked and I had to fight back tears because I had thought exactly that for the last few days, that I was just a fling.

"Am I? How do you think I got this? And where do you think she is? Huh?"

"I... I don't know."

"She gave this to me, that night your little friend came by and dropped it off. Told me all about it, but said that hearing you say you actually loved her, having to say it back, it made her sick. She told me to bond you, make you submit, put you in your place so she could find hers and then she left."

I couldn't hold back the tears anymore, they fell freely like the words spilling from Cameron's lips that I didn't want to hear. I felt like I was dying as I slipped to the floor, my heart definitely broken in two now, like I would bleed out right there in his living room. Suddenly, that was all I wanted to do, just end it all and have it over with, not have to hurt anymore, or for the rest of my life. I kneeled there crying and apparently feeling like he managed to break me enough that I wouldn't move anytime soon, Cameron left the room and headed to the kitchen.

He didn't plan on the fact that, Frost or no Frost, I still hated him and had no intention of being stuck with him forever. I wiped away the tears enough that I could see properly and took stock of the room, then did the only thing I could. I was on my feet, across the room and had barreled through the plate window before he even realized I had moved. I rolled through the impact on the other side and then sprang to my feet and bolted into the dark woods, knowing he would be on my heels in moments. Branches caught in my hair and ripped at my arms and legs but I didn't care, I could see well enough to avoid falling and that was all I cared about as I ran. I was at full speed, but I could hear him behind me, closing in, he would catch me before I got where I was headed, the only place I could think to go, the place I always met Frost.

I was so close to that special spot that I could smell the lavender we had planted in the little glade the year before. It made me push myself just a little harder, but it wasn't enough, I felt the air forced from my lungs as Cameron barreled into my back, knocking me off my feet. I landed hard, face first in the dirt and leaf rot of the forest floor, still frozen enough that I felt the cuts as they ripped open on my left cheek and my lower lip. He shifted his weight and turned me over then pinned me to the ground and growled in my face, his eyes wild and angry.

He was pissed, and as much as I hated him, he had the right to be, his mate had run and that was a severe offense in our world. I closed my eyes, still crying but fighting the fear that threatened to make me freeze up. If I let it take hold, he would be able to tell, to smell it and feel it and he would use it against me. I clenched my jaw and tried shoving down the edges of panic and unravel the knot in my stomach. I swallowed against the bile rising in my throat as he leaned closer than I was comfortable with and fought off the rising urge to just shift and bite the hell out of him. That wouldn't end well for me and I knew it. I was running rapid-fire through my options and trying to decide what to do, how I could get away from him when suddenly, his weight was gone from over me. In a flicker of moonlight and the sound of snapping jaws he vanished and it took me a moment to regain my bearings. I pulled to my feet and realized that it wasn't moonlight I had seen, but a flash of white fur, gleaming like silver in the darkness. My breath caught and a sound that mimicked my wolf's whimper left my lips, causing the stark-white wolf to turn around and face me.

Those violet eyes stripped me down to my soul and as she approached me, I dropped to my knees and wrapped my arms around her, holding on for dear life. I looked over her shoulder to where Cameron was splayed out, knocked unconscious, and knew he would be out for a little while. I pulled my white wolf closer and cried into her neck, her soft fur tickling my nose as I nuzzled her, my fingers working through the pristine coat.

After a few moments she pulled away and I whined, reaching for her as she moved away behind a small stand of trees. She came back a few moments later, human and clothed and fell into my arms, pulling me close and holding me. We allowed ourselves those few minutes just sitting there holding each other not speaking, but then we knew we had to move before her brother woke up. We stood together and made our way deeper into the woods, knowing that we couldn't conceal our scent trail but that we could at least put some distance between us and figure out what to do. I let her fall in a couple steps ahead of me, just looking at her as my brain worked over the last week and what had happened. I couldn't help but smile as I watched her run, knowing that I had a lot of questions for her that needed answers but content to just stare at her for a little while.

She was just as stunning as she always had been at five foot six, only an inch taller than me, still sporting that shoulder-length flash of pale blonde hair and those eyes that stopped my heart when she looked at me. As if she read my mind, she glanced over her shoulder, settling those eyes on mine and for a moment, I forgot what I had been thinking about and had to regain my mind. She saw me shake my head to clear it and smiled at me, having seen me do it so many times that she knew exactly what had just happened. That smile, it killed me and she knew it too, perfect lips, full, just slightly pouty, just as soft as they looked. She was slim, toned but not skinny and had just the right amount of curves in just the right places.

We finally stopped and I was so distracted that I almost ran right into her, but pulled up just in time to keep from colliding. We were on the edge of Clipper territory and I wondered why she had stopped but figured this worked just fine for talking and finding out what was going on.

"I got your letter." The words were soft, like her words often were, spoken so gently that a decent breeze would wash them away and I held fast to keep from melting on the spot.

"Yeah, and then gave it to Cameron." Remembering what he had told me made my eyes narrow slightly and the words come out clipped and sharp. I'd let the whole conversation with her brother slip from my mind when I'd seen her, honestly just relieved to see her again. I'd been so caught up with having her close that I'd allowed the feeling to consume me like usual, but now it all came rushing back.

"I didn't give it to him, Kyndle. He found it. God he was livid, I was terrified he would kill me. So I ran."

Her voice was small, pained and she was staring at the ground, her brow knit and a frown on her face as she let out a ragged sigh.

"And why didn't you come to me then? You weren't at school, no calls, no texts, no notes or letters. Nothing Frost."

I watched her profile in the dark as she squeezed her eyes closed tight for a moment before she brushed her hair back and looked up at me.

"I didn't have my phone with me, or a way to get you a letter." I opened my mouth to respond, but she stopped me cold when she raised a hand and I snapped my mouth shut again and let her finish. "I tried to come to school, to come see you, but Cameron must have told Dane about the letter. The patrols around Clipper land have gotten intense. I couldn't get through, even for classes, they kept chasing me away."

"So... You don't want me to be with him? You didn't say I made you sick?"

Just repeating the things that Cameron had said such a short time ago made the tears I had been fighting start again. The first tear hadn't even made it all the way down my cheek before she had me in against her, one arm around my waist, the other hand wiping my tears away. I didn't even think twice, didn't question and didn't hesitate, the moment I felt her near me, touching me, my arms went around her, holding her tight and refusing to let go.

"God no. Oh Kyndle, did he tell you that?"

I nodded and felt another burst of tears fall, feeling silly for crying so much recently but figured love does weird things to people.

"He said you wanted to be free of me so you could take your place in a pack like I should..." The already quiet words were muffled even further against her shoulder and she hugged me tighter against her.

"Baby, listen to me, my brother is a grade A jerk. He'd say anything to keep us apart. I love you. When I heard that you were being given to him for bonding, I felt like I was dying. I hurt so much and I was trying to figure out how to see you when I got your letter and everything fell apart."

"You really love me?" There was a small, whimpering tone to my voice that I would have been embarrassed about had anyone other than Frost heard it. I knew she wouldn't judge me for it though and I wasn't ashamed of letting her know how much thinking I'd lost her had broken me. She leaned back a little and looked at me, those pale purple eyes locked on mine.

"Of course I do. Kyndle, I've loved you since the day I met you almost seven years ago. All I wanna do is spend the rest of my life with you." That just managed to cause a whole new flood of completely useless and unwelcome tears, this was getting ridiculous. She pulled me back in and I smiled through the tears and turned my face into her neck.

"I feel the same. But it's too late, the bonding ceremony was tonight." I felt her go still in my arms, everything, even her breathing stopped and her muscles tensed then I felt her exhale sharply against my shoulder. "Baby?" I asked, my tone gentle so I wouldn't startle her out of whatever thoughts she had slipped into.

"We'll figure this out honey. There's a way, there has to be. I have an idea, but I need you to trust me." There was a pleading in her tone as she spoke to me that threatened to break me.

"I do." I replied and I felt the movement when she smiled against my shoulder at my words and broke out in my own in response.

"Do you have your phone?" I nodded against her shoulder when she asked and then moved enough to hand it to her and she unlocked it and grinned when she apparently got service.

She messed with it for a few minutes, pausing for short spurts here and there then swiping and tapping away again before she finally locked it and handed it back to me. I didn't bother to ask, I did trust her. Completely despite having let that trust waver some recently.

I simply slipped the phone back in my pocket, a little shocked it had managed to survive my escape, capture and rescue. She checked the watch I was wearing and then grabbed my hand and tugged me along after her as she walked through the trees. We walked for a few minutes and then came to the road, stood and waited, though I wasn't sure what for. That is, until a familiar pickup truck pulled to the side of the road and we both ran over and hopped into the back seat.

"Hey bestie! I see you found your girl. Dunno how well you remember me, I'm Abbey."

"I do remember you, even if I didn't, Kyndle talks about you all the time. Frost. Good to officially meet you." Abbey nodded her agreement to the statement and I just sat silently as they discussed where we were going. "We need to head south east. The last few months I've been in contact with the Alpha of the Sunshine pack, he'll help us."

"Sunshine pack?" What kind of hippies were we on our way to meet and where on earth were they, that's what I wanted to know.

"Yes love, Sunshine pack. They're in Northern California and are a very modern pack, progressive. Alpha pair are both male, they'll help us out if they can."

Abbey smiled at Frost and I nodded a little as I slid over into my girlfriends space without another word, unwilling to let her get too far away from me for too long. She shifted around a little and then made me lay down, resting my head in her lap as she ran her fingers through my hair, picking twigs and pine needles out of it and lulling me to sleep in a matter of seconds. For the first time in more days than I cared to admit, there was no panic to my sleep, no restlessness, no fleeting, flickering images of Frost. There was just sleep, sound, deep sleep with the smell of my mate surrounding me, holding me tight.

CHAPTER NINE

I WOKE to the feeling of the truck decelerating and had to blink a few times to remember where I was and what was happening. The moment I regained my senses and Frost's scent hit me it all came back. We were in some serious trouble and yet I couldn't manage to make myself worry right that moment, not with my white wolf so close to me, she eased all those fears, calmed my worries. I sat up, stretched and yawned as I looked around, wondering where on earth we were as I scanned the area. It was either still dark, or had managed to get dark again, I really wasn't sure which and that was a little bit worrying.

"Abbey drove all day, you must have been exhausted, you slept for almost eighteen hours love."

"How do you do that?"

"Do what?"

"Read my mind like that... You do it a lot."

She just shrugged and smiled at me and I knew that would be all the reply I would get, at least for now. Okay so, I knew her almost as well as she knew me, maybe just as well, at least I hoped I did. "So where are we then?"

"Just outside Ranger pack land. I wasn't going to make it

much further without sleep and food, even Frost was starting to look a little ragged."

I glanced over at my mate as my best friend finished speaking and noticed how tired she looked. I slid out of the truck and helped Frost and Abbey unload the camping gear out of the bed of the truck. We set up the tent in silence, my two saviors exhausted and myself, well, I was still processing everything that had happened in the last seven days. I suddenly felt like I could sleep for the next week and still not be caught up on what I had missed since that horrid evening in my parents' house. I sighed and it merged into a yawn that made Frost giggle a little despite the weariness I could see behind her eyes. I shrugged a little and she just nodded toward the tent, making me smile then wander over to it.

The three of us crawled into the thing, which was actually bigger than it had seemed, large enough to sleep at least ten people with dividers separating out three distinct 'rooms' from each other. I said goodnight to Abbey, thanking her at least three more times for her part in getting me away from Cameron. I was still slightly shaken up over what had happened, and what had almost happened out there in the woods, but I was trying to keep it hidden. I should have known better than that after two years with Frost, should have known that she would see right through me and my charade.

"Hey. Talk to me baby."

Her voice was soft as usual as she pulled me in close against her side and I cuddled up, my head resting on her shoulder, eyes closed. I just shook my head, not wanting to get into it right then, just wanting to sleep a little more and pretend that none of it had happened.

"Kyn, sweetie, you need to talk about it."

"I will Frost, I promise just, not right now. I'm still exhausted and so are you, I can see it, feel it. You need sleep."

She let out a small sigh that was laced with exasperation but then I felt her nod a little bit, admitting I was right. I shifted enough to bury my face lightly against the side of her neck, traced a few small kisses toward her jawline and then nuzzled the soft spot just behind and below her ear. She let out a little purr, the noise even more adorable when she was in human form, but having the same effect on me in either form.

"Keep that up and we won't get any sleep." Her tone was playful but laced with a heated desire that matched my own, a desire that neither of us was in the position to do anything about just then. So I took the road rarely traveled between us and decided to behave myself, returned my head to her shoulder, tightened my arm around her waist and closed my eyes, letting the easy sleep that only came when I was in her arms overtake me.

The sounds of birds singing outside the tent woke me gently from my sleep, the sun hitting the sides of the thin tan walls and lending the inside a bit of a glow. Warmth began seeping into the space, heating it even further, but not enough to drag me away from Frost's arms. I loved waking up with her, we'd only had the opportunity to spend an entire night together a total of three times in the two years we'd been together. This made number four and knowing that I didn't have to jump up and rush home made it so much more special than the others. I could settle in, snuggle up close and lay there for a little while, wrapped up in my mate's arms. My real mate, not that jerk I was forced to bond with the day before. I didn't let that thought linger very long, not wanting to deal with thinking about what had taken place so early in the day.

I felt Frost shift slightly behind me and just cuddled in closer against her, knowing that it would take her a few more minutes to actually wake up. Her arms tightened around me and I let out a happy little sigh before I pulled one of her hands up and kissed the backs of her fingers. I let my eyes close again and sank back into a light sleep, perfectly content to lay there and drift between reality and my dreams until she was awake. It was almost an hour later when I felt a scattering of small kisses being trailed down the back of my neck and just smiled. My beautiful wolf sure knew how to wake a girl up and I stretched a little, arching my back against her until it popped slightly and then turned in her arms. I opened my eyes slowly and smiled up at her as she returned the smile down at me, her hands tracing up and down my spine lightly.

"Morning."

"Mmm, morning love." My voice was still a little raspy and I yawned as I finished saying the words then giggled a little.

"How did you sleep?"

"Better than I have in a while. You?"

"Same. Ready to get moving? Abbey's been up for a while from the sound of things."

I tuned in and heard what Frost was talking about, the sounds of a morning fire crackling and camp pans clanging as my best friend made breakfast. Moments later the smell of sausage and bacon assaulted me and my stomach rumbled loudly to remind me that I hadn't eaten in a very long time. I gave Frost a quick kiss and then slipped from her arms and into the slightly-chilled morning air inside the tent, shivering a bit until I adjusted. Once I was back in my jeans and a long-sleeved tee shirt I pulled my shoes on and checked to make sure Frost was dressed. We exited the tent together and found Abbey deep in concentration over a pan of rapidly scrambling eggs.

I couldn't help but laugh a little at the look on her face, brow furrowed a bit, the tip of her tongue sticking out of the right side of her mouth. She looked hilarious and the face she made at me when she realized that I was laughing at her only made me laugh harder. It must have been infectious because in moments Frost was laughing and it was only seconds later that Abbey started as well. We composed ourselves in just enough time to save breakfast from being burned and then settled in around the fire to eat and finish waking up. Once the food had vanished, we set to work, each with a job to do, Frost packing up supplies, Abbey loading the truck while I took the dishes down to the nearby creek and washed them so they could be packed up again. I couldn't help but be impressed that Abbey had been so prepared on such short notice, but then, that was Abbey. I smiled as I finished cleaning the dishes and then hauled them all back toward the spot where we had camped.

A light breeze kicked up and wafted across my body and I stopped dead in my tracks, my pulse notching up as the scent the wind carried hit me. I took a deep breath and kept myself from falling into a panic then started toward camp again, just barely keeping myself from running the whole way. I ignored the greetings spoken my direction by my mate and my best friend and just pulled open the back door, threw the freshly cleaned dishes into the truck and then turned toward them, meeting confused looks.

"We need to go, now."

"Baby, what's wrong? You look like you saw a ghost..."

"Your brother is out there. Somehow he followed us."

The two women in front of me looked stunned and I could tell that they were about to panic on me.

"Relax, he's not about to come at me with you two right here. Let's just get this stuff tied down, get in the truck and get out of here as quick as we can."

They both nodded, tied down the cargo in record time and then we were in the truck and back on the road.

"You're sure it was him?"

"Yeah Abbey, I'm sure. I'd know that scent anywhere after the last couple days."

She just nodded and didn't question further, she knew that if I said I'd caught his scent then I had, I wasn't about to lie. We stayed on the road until we were all desperately in need of a bathroom break and our stomachs were growling and then Abbey pulled into a truck stop. We dealt with our needs, taking our food to go, then hopped back in the truck and started out again, me behind the wheel, Frost in the passenger seat beside me and Abbey stretched out on the backseat eating her burger and fries. We weren't far from our destination now thanks to Abbey driving most of the night, even though we had tried to not make ourselves easy to follow by taking some rather circuitous routes when needed.

I drove the last leg of our trip which landed us just outside Crescent City, California where Frost contacted Barkley and Hank, the Alpha pair of the Sunshine pack. It was a decent day, sitting in the mid-fifties and a far cry from the rather bleak snow that we had left behind. It was a bit amazing to me how quickly a love of snow could be turned on its head when it was mixed with bad memories. Barkley gave us directions to a clearing just outside the Klamath National Forest and we agreed to meet there. It didn't take us long to make it thanks to Abbey's amazing sense of direction and we waited for her to park the truck then hopped out to meet the new Alphas. I took the lead as the pair entered the clearing, what looked to be the higher wolves in their pack behind them. Normally I would feel trapped in such a situation, definitely given the twenty or so wolves with the pair, but for some reason I was completely at ease with this group.

A large man standing about six foot five with a shock of blond hair cropped just above his ears and the clearest green eyes I'd ever seen approached us. His smile was warm and genuine and I instantly felt like I was among friends when he offered me his hand and introduced himself as Barkley.

"I'm Kyndle. It's good to meet you."

I shook his hand and then Abbey follow suit before he introduced us to his mate, Hank and we both shook his hand as well, having met Frost before, they both hugged her. The pair introduced us to their beta, her mate and their three teenage children and then to a few of their older pack members. The led us a little further into the area to a spot where they had set up a few tables and some chairs and already had a fire going, ready for a little friendly cookout. It all seemed so relaxed and laid back and I couldn't help but feel completely at home despite never having met any of this group before that day.

"So, Frost tells us that you're in a bit of a tight spot honey."

Hank had the deepest voice I had ever heard and was probably the only person I'd seen that could make Barkley look small. He was a sturdy six foot nine inches and built like a brick wall with the tight curls of red hair that matched the slight Irish accent I could catch when he spoke. His facial hair, a full beard that was cropped close and perfectly trimmed was the same color as his hair. His sparkling dark green eyes were full of laughter and kindness and I had the distinct feeling that he could make anyone feel like they belonged despite his imposing size.

"A tight spot... That's putting it, well, mildly." I rolled my eyes a little as Barkley and Hank glanced at each other and each raised an eyebrow then looked back to me.

"Spill, we said we would help and we'll do what we can."

"Okay, where to begin..."

I decided that the beginning was the best place to start and just let the story spill out, telling them everything that had happened over the last couple years, covering all of the sneaking around, lying and hiding that Frost and I had been forced to live through. By the time I finished walking through it all, ending with smelling Cameron in the clearing earlier that day, Frost was sitting right beside me, her arm around my waist. I leaned my head on her shoulder and let out a heavy sigh as I watched Barkley shake his head a bit and whisper something to Hank. They asked us to wait for a moment and then left the table with Faith, their Beta, and spoke privately for a few minutes.

When they returned, they settled back into their seats and Hank gave Frost and I a small smile that told us more than any words could. They couldn't get me away from Cameron, couldn't break the bond that had been made and my heart threatened to break right there on the spot. I held it together to wait and see what they had to say, maybe I was misreading the look, maybe they could do something.

"Okay girls, there's good news and bad news. Which do you want first?" It was Barkley who finally spoke and I took a deep breath and exhaled slowly then let myself speak as I hoped that my voice wouldn't waver.

"Good."

"Okay, the good news is, there is a way out, a way to get you out of this bond." I almost jumped up and cheered but then I remembered that there was bad news as well and steadied myself to receive it.

"And the bad news?"

"The bad news..."

Faith had started to speak and I took the moment to look at her, actually look at her, for the first time, taking in her jet-black hair and deep brown eyes. She looked nothing like either of her Alphas and was dwarfed by them at only five foot five inches tall. She paused for a moment as she looked over at her leaders for the okay to finish telling us what we needed to know and Barkley gave her a small nod.

"...Is that we can't help you. No one can. The only one that can get you out from under this bond you've found yourself in... Is you."

CHAPTER TEN

"ME? HOW? I mean, I didn't want this bond in the first place, I would know if I could just walk away, wouldn't I?"

The three looked at each other as if trying to decide who would be answering me and after a moment of unspoken exchange, Barkley continued.

"You wouldn't know about this. Elders don't speak of it and most Alphas refuse to acknowledge that it ever happened, much less still happens. You have to challenge him."

"Challenge? Like, fight him? One on one?" I looked between the three of them and they all nodded as they confirmed my words and I turned my gaze toward Frost who looked as shocked as I felt. She was even more pale than usual, and her light eyes were misted over and unfocused, telltale signs she was fighting the urge to cry. "Baby…" The word left my lips as barely more than a whisper but it was enough to snap her out of the trance she had slipped into and she looked at me.

"You can't, Kyn. You can't fight him, he's twice your size!"

I just nodded a little and pulled her into my arms, hugging her as the tears she had been fighting began to fall.

She buried her face in my shoulder and cried, her own shoulders shaking as she sobbed and I just rubbed her back, still in shock and not feeling much of anything. I looked at Barkley and Hank and they both looked pained, like they had hoped that they could offer more help than they had.

"We're so sorry, Kyndle. It's the only way to break the bond. He has to die and it has to be you that does it. We can be of more help once that step is completed but the best we can do until then is support you and help you train. Hank and I are more than happy to spar with you for a few weeks, we're both bigger than your male and if you can learn to best us then you have a better chance against him."

I just nodded a little bit and Frost finally pushed back from me, her eyes ringed in red and her cheeks streaked with tears.

"No. Kyndle, please, don't do this."

"I have to, Frost. I can't be tied to him forever; you know what it'll do to me."

"He'll kill you." She looked at the ground as she spoke and my heart broke at the pain in her voice, she was terrified that she would lose me forever.

"No, he won't." She shook her head as she looked up at me, about to argue with me but I put a finger on her lips to stop her from speaking. "Frost, don't try to talk me out of this. I have to do it, there's no other way. And once I do, we can be together. No more hiding, no more sneaking around, no more fear. I'll challenge him, and I will win. For you... For us."

She searched my eyes for a moment and then pulled my hand away from her mouth and gave me a small smile. She knew as well as I did that this would be a fight from beginning to end, but that I would do it for us, so we could be together. I finally looked at Abbey and it was clear that she had cried too and I reached out for her and she joined us at the table. I hugged her and she hugged me back, tighter than she had in years and I felt her choke back a small sob.

"I'll be okay. I won't challenge him until I think I'm ready, okay?" That was meant for she and Frost both and I looked between them until they both nodded and then looked back to Hank and Barkley with a nod. "Let's do this."

"Then we start now."

Barkley nodded to Faith who smiled and stood from the table then walked into the middle of the clearing and started strip off her clothes.

"You'll fight Faith first, she's your size but being about fifteen years older her wolf will be bigger than yours. From there you will move on to her mate, Justin, then to Justin's brother Kyle, one of our scouts and then to me and finally on to Hank. Make it through us all and you'll be ready to take on your problem Alpha, here's hoping it goes quickly."

I nodded and moved to join Faith in the clearing, starting to work out of my own clothes as she shifted in front of me, the average sized woman replaced by a massive black wolf with deep chocolate eyes. She was at least two inches taller than me at the shoulder and I watched her move for a moment before shifting myself. My wolf senses kicked in after paws met earth and I turned my gaze on Faith across the clearing.

She lowered her head and loosed a growl in my direction and I responded in kind as she launched herself at me. She was taller, heavier and fast as hell, but I was an Alpha where she was only a Beta and there was only about twenty minutes of growling, snapping jaws and yelps before I had her pinned to the ground, my teeth brushing her spine through her thick fur. She whined to voice that she conceded to me and I released her, crossed the clearing and shifted back as I reached for my clothes. I was breathing a bit hard but as Faith shifted back. I could tell she was breathing harder and was a bit worse for wear than I was. We both pulled our clothes back on and Barkley sauntered up with a smirk, dropped his arm across Faith's shoulders and gave me an approving nod. "Good job, little Alpha, very good job. What do you think Faith?"

"She's strong, no doubt about that, wish I could say that I was holding back, but she rather efficiently kicked my ass. She's quick, strong and smart on her feet. Give her a couple hours or so then toss her in with Justin."

He nodded and I couldn't help but grin a little and feel just a tad proud of myself for the performance I had just put in. I had a moment to wonder if I would fare as well against Justin but then pushed the thought aside, I needed to believe I could do it if I was going to make an effort toward this goal. I had just pulled my shoes back on when someone shouted that food was ready and we all migrated back toward the tables situated around the fire pit. The smells of hamburgers, hot dogs, chicken and steaks filled the clearing mingled with the underlying scents of grilled vegetables and potatoes.

Abbey, Frost and I settled at a table with Barkley, Hank, Faith and Justin after we'd filled plates with various foods and we all ate in relative silence. As we got closer to clearing our plates and began to chat again, other members of the pack started to filter into the clearing and join the cookout. Before long all seventy or so pack members were present. There was chatter going on all over the clearing, children running around playing, teens lingering along the edges laughing and listening to music and the overall feel was one of family. I marveled at how happy and comfortable with each other the large pack seemed to be and wondered if the Clippers had ever been like this. If they had, it was long before I was born and probably even before my parents were born since none of their generation ever mentioned anything like this. I just ate slowly and smiled as I watched the group mix and mingle together, enjoying the food and the company.

Once we finished eating, we dragged our chairs over by the fire and I was just about to bring one up between Frost and Abbey when I felt a hand on my wrist. I turned to find my white wolf with her hand gripping my wrist lightly and smiled at her as she tugged me over and then settled me in her lap. I wasn't about to argue with her and just cuddled in as she wrapped her arms around me and I leaned my head on her shoulder. The group started roasting marshmallows and I declined when offered a roasting fork, content to join the conversation and stay right there in Frost's lap. The sun set and once the chatter and laughter settled down a bit Barkley looked my way and raised an eyebrow at me. "You ready for round two?" I grinned at him and nodded, ready for whatever they threw at me after the evening we had shared with the pack.

It had taken that hour sitting in Frost's lap, her arms around me, her scent enveloping me, to make me sure that I could do what needed to be done. I wouldn't lose her, couldn't give her up and would do whatever I had to do to have her in my life forever. I slipped from her lap and moved into the clearing behind where the gathering was set up, the darkness not bothering me in the least. I began stripping off my clothes as Justin stepped into the clearing and started doing the same, neither of us showing any shame or shyness at the action. Werewolves were typically lacking in shyness when it came to nudity, having to strip down to shift if we held any hope of having clothes to put back on later. I studied him a bit, taking him in and guessed he was about five foot ten with deep brown hair and remembered his hazel eyes. I watched as he shifted, his wolf bigger than Faith's, definitely bigger than mine and actually even bigger than Cameron's. He was at least five inches taller at the shoulder than my wolf and was solid, heavy but looked like he might not be as agile as I was.

Even I had to admit he was a handsome wolf, deep brown with a hint of reddish highlighting that glinted in the firelight and piercing hazel eyes that picked up the yellow of the fire and gleamed almost gold in the darkness. I stared for a moment and then shifted, my own pale cinnamon wolf making the younger wolves that had joined the cookout after my tangle with Faith gasp and start to whisper. I was an odd and striking color, I knew that much, but I wasn't used to such a reaction and I turned pale blue eyes on the small group of teens and cocked my head to one side slightly. They all smiled and a few even laughed at my very canine reaction to them and then I turned my attention back to Justin. I barely had time to focus on him before he rushed me and I planted my paws, waiting for him to close the gap. He barreled down on me and everything else faded into the background, vanished from my senses and I drew all my attention to the wolf coming at me.

He was just about to plow into me when I moved, sidestepping just slightly and catching his side with my teeth. It wasn't enough to do any serious damage, but did managed to tear a yelp from him and leave the slightly metallic taste of blood on my tongue. He slid to a stop and turned on me, a snarl pulling his lips back from his teeth as he growled in my direction. I had pissed him off, good, that was what I wanted, it would make him reactive rather than thinking and he would make mistakes. It was a tactic that I hoped to use against Cameron since he had a temper on him that was easy to provoke.

Justin charged again and after several minutes tangling together he managed to pin me on my back, his jaws headed for my throat. I wasn't about to let it end so easily and I planted my back paws in his gut and kicked, sending him rolling to the side and I pounced on him before he could recover. He got loose and we fought across the clearing for what felt like ages but couldn't have been more than another thirty minutes.

I was starting to get tired and I hoped it wouldn't make me careless, thankfully it seemed like he was as well and I took advantage of that. Another five minutes and I had his larger bulk pinned under me, his stomach against the dirt and his paws splayed out in a way that kept him from getting them back underneath him. I grabbed him by the scruff and held on as he fought then, after deciding that I was done with his struggling, yanked a bit roughly on the skin between my teeth and he yelped then stopped struggling. I let him go after a few moments to a round of clapping and cheering then returned to my clothes, shifted back and got dressed again as Justin did the same. "I admit, I'm a little shocked." The voice made me turn with my shoes in hand and grin at Justin who was pulling his shirt down into place. "I not only didn't expect you to last that long but I definitely didn't expect you to beat me."

"I told you she's good." Faith was smirking at her mate as

he shook his head and I just laughed a little at the pair of them, knowing that I had one more fairly simple opponent and then I'd be on to the big boys.

"Well thank you both, thankfully I grew up with brothers who didn't pull their punches, or their bites. I learned to protect myself young." They both nodded and then stepped back as Barkley stepped up beside me and smiled, obviously impressed with my performance as well.

"You held up nicely, tomorrow we'll put you up against Kyle, see how you do with him and then we'll go from there." I nodded a little and then laughed when Frost wrapped her arms around me and picked me up, she was a lot stronger than she looked, we all were. I slipped my arms around her neck and hugged her back as the group looked on, all smiling at us as we embraced. "It's nice to see two Alphas enjoy each other so much. We're a rarity when it comes to Alpha pairs." Barkley indicated himself and Hank and I had to admit that they were, it wasn't often we saw Alphas who actually liked each other, much less were in love.

"It's been a while since I met an Alpha pair that was together because they wanted to be, not because they had to be. It's really sad actually." He and Hank nodded their agreement and then he handed me a slip of paper with an address on it and invited us to stay with them.

"No point in getting a room in town, who knows how long you'll be in the area and it's easier if you're close so we can work with you."

I nodded, agreeing with the thought and then Frost and Abbey did the same and we rejoined the group for the end of the campfire roasting and song session. It was well after three in the morning before we doused the fire, packed up and headed back to the land the pack owned. There were a couple empty houses in the development they had set up so Barkley and Hank set us up in one of them for the duration of our stay with their pack. Abbey set herself up in the downstairs bedroom, she had always hated dealing with stairs and that left Frost and I in the master bedroom.

We unpacked the few things that we had and then collapsed onto the king-sized bed, thankful for the chance to get a full night of sleep. She settled in on her back, her left arm up behind her head and I cuddled up against her right side which prompted her to wrap her arm around me and smile, her eyes closed. We laid there for a while, my right arm draped across her stomach, her fingers tracing little patterns on my back. No words were spoken, neither of us felt the need, it was so rare we had nights together and now we'd managed to get two in a row, and more to come. We weren't interested in doing our usual chatting because now we had time, all the time in the world if things worked out our way, and I had the feeling they would.

I cuddled in closer as a yawn slipped out and felt her laugh a little. I slapped her stomach lightly and closed my eyes, letting myself fall into the feel of her against me. I knew I could definitely get used to the way this felt and I prayed that we would never be apart again. It was with that thought floating through my head that I drifted off to sleep, knowing that she wouldn't be far behind me.

My dreams were usually few and far between and typically something completely unbelievable but that night they were far too close to reality and far too intense for my liking. I was in a clearing, the full moon overhead and the early spring breeze blowing the smells of flowering plants around me. I was in wolf form, my point of view and sharper senses giving that away, I never dreamed myself in wolf form, ever. The reality of being a wolf was so much better than dreaming it was that my dream state never bothered to try and reproduce it. Here I was though, in a dream, as a wolf and I was unsettled, even asleep, then it hit me why. One of the scents I was picking up on was familiar and as I my gaze tracked across the field, I was standing in I saw him. Cameron stood there, tall, proud, daring me to come at him and I paused for only a split second before charging the bigger wolf before me.

He was ready and countered my move, leaving me scrambling to regain my footing and balance as I whirled mid-charge to face him again. I was too slow and he barreled into me, knocking me off my feet and pinning me to the earth, snarling at me. The look in his eyes was pure murder, he was angry. He wouldn't stop until I was either begging him to let me live with the promise of being his mate forever or dead at his feet. My pulse raced, my heart trying to hammer its way out of my chest as I looked up into that cold gaze, knowing that I was at the end.

He shifted to human form and pressed me down into the dirt beneath me, his hand tight around my neck and I whimpered and shifted back as well. "Give in and give me what I want. Stop fighting me. Be my mate. Submit!" I felt myself tense and wasn't sure if it was in my dream or my real body tensing as my resolve kicked in and my jaw set.

"Fuck off."

The words slipped out as a growl in the face of my attacker and would be mate and those two words infuriated him even further. I hadn't even seen him get his hand on a weapon, but the piercing pain that ripped through my side told me I'd been stabbed. I let out a scream of pain as he twisted the blade and heated pain shot up my spine as everything faded around me and I slipped into darkness. A scream pierced the dark and it took me a few moments to realize that it was mine and that I was being shaken. I felt a panic like I'd never experienced grip me and my eyes snapped open. I was breathing hard and covered in a cold sweat as I took in the unfamiliar room in the faint sunlight filtering through the curtains.

CHAPTER ELEVEN

"BABY! IT'S okay, I'm right here... Shhh."

Frost's voice silenced the screams and I looked up at her, fear and panic etched across her features. I started to come to my senses, my breathing still ragged and frantic and my heart racing. I whimpered as I crawled over to my mate and curled myself into her. It was a pitiful sight surely, but I couldn't help it. The dream had scared me to the point that I couldn't manage anything other than sitting in her lap, shivering and glad that it had only been a dream. She held me, silent strength wrapped around me as I calmed down and when I finally shifted away and looked at her, concern was etched across her features.

"Are you okay sweetheart?" The worry tinged her voice and for a moment all I could do was nod a little. I hated that I had upset her, but I was unable to get past what I had seen in my dream without a little time to process. She didn't push, didn't try to make me talk and didn't tell me I needed to get it out, just sat there quietly until I gathered myself and managed a solid, steady breath.

"Nightmare, really bad one." I finally got out and she just gave me a small nod and waited for me to decide I was ready to tell her more. After a few moments I felt my brow furrow as I tried to urge myself past what I was still seeing flickering through my mind. "Cameron was there, he challenged me, pinned me and then he..." I trailed off, knowing that the dream could have ended worse but that it hadn't exactly been something she would enjoy hearing. "He stabbed me, I think he pierced my heart. I... I died, Frost."

I started to shake again and she just pulled me back in and kissed the top of my head right about the time I heard a sniff from near the door. I looked over to see Abbey standing in the open doorway, crying and my heart broke again, I had terrified the two most important people in my life.

"I'm sorry, I heard you screaming and rushed in to make sure you were okay."

I just nodded, glad that she had bothered worrying about me, but I never had any doubt that she worried, she always had and probably always would. Frost continued to rub my back and I finally settled down again but then realized that I couldn't sit still, I needed to move. I slipped out of the bed and over to the window, throwing back the curtains and wincing slightly in the bright light. I turned and cast a glance at the bedside table, it was after two in the afternoon and I had been asleep for almost nine hours.

I sure didn't feel like I had been out that long and actually felt like I could sleep for another three or four if given the chance to let my mind relax again. I sighed and made my way back to the bed, not sitting back down, just taking Frost's outstretched hand and giving it a squeeze.

"Come on, it's later than I thought, we should find Barkley and Hank and get moving on the next step of this training that they have in store for me. The quicker I'm ready, the sooner Cameron is dealt with and the less time I have to deal with these damn dreams."

I gave the other two women with me a half-hearted smile and then swapped clothes into my jeans and a tank top and made my way out of the house. It was time to take the next step toward meeting my destiny and whatever that might entail and I was as ready as I could expect to be. Frost and Abbey caught up to me after a couple minutes and a few moments later we found the two men that we were looking for and exchanged greetings. Within a couple minutes we were loaded into Abbey's truck following the pair with Faith, Justin and Kyle in a car behind us.

We pulled up to the clearing we had been in the day before and piled out of the vehicles, giving the space a once over. It looked a lot different without the cookout clutter set up and I felt at peace in the space, glad for the reprieve from my nerves for a few moments. Kyle gave me a few seconds to myself and then walked over and slapped me on the shoulder, getting my attention. I looked over at him and managed a smile, noting that he seemed completely ready for what was about to happen. I only wished that I was, that I felt as confident in myself and my abilities as I had been the day before with Faith and Justin. That dream had worked me over and done a number on my self-confidence as well as my mental state, I was a bit of a mess. I sighed as he crossed the clearing and started stripping down to shift, readying for the spar we had ahead of us.

I looked over and realized that more members of the pack had filtered into the clearing to watch the training fight. They were all interested in watching what I would do with Kyle after what had happened with Justin the day before. I shook my head and tried to focus on what needed to be done as Kyle shifted across the space from me. His wolf was the same white blond as his hair and sported the same watery green eyes as well, not to mention being big. His human form was six foot one and his wolf was massive, I could only imagine what Barkley and Hank looked like. The thought made me shiver a little and I had to give myself a little mental pep talk to get my ass in gear. I stripped and shifted then turned to face my new opponent, knowing that this one would be a lot tougher than the last two. I might outrank Kyle but he was still a huge bulk of wolf that I had no chance of overpowering, I would have to outsmart him.

He charged, and I reacted, starting off decent but not lasting and the fight only managed to go on for about ten minutes before he had me pinned. I whined my consent to his victory and he let me up so I could return to the group and Barkley gave me a little pep talk which actually helped bolster me a little bit. I decided to try again and turned to face the big blond wolf once more, trotting a few feet toward him and then planting my paws. I was determined to stand steady and let him come to me but that all went out the window after about five minutes of staring each other down. I huffed and charged at him and he took advantage of my impatience, landing me pinned on my back in just nine minutes. I was ticked off and everyone could tell when I snapped at him as he let me up and he turned on me with a snarl and a snap of his jaws.

Hank stepped between us and grabbed me as I lunged for the larger wolf, carrying me back to my side of the clearing as if I was a Labrador puppy and not a wolf the size of a pony. I huffed as he dropped me on my furry ass and grumbled a little as he gave me a bit of a stern reprimand before offering some advice.

"Stop being so impatient. It doesn't ever work in your favor and anyone who has known you for more than a few minutes will try to exploit it. Get it under control and stop letting it dictate the way you fight and how you move."

I calmed down enough to take the words he offered me, relaxed again by the time Frost stepped up to me. "Hey beautiful." She squatted down and leaned her forehead against mine as she scratched behind my ears and I gave her a little happy wolf noise for her efforts. "You can do this love, I know you can, just keep calm, be patient and don't let your temper get the better of you. I believe in you, Kyndle, and I love you." She kissed my nose and I nuzzled her neck before I turned my attention back to Kyle, knowing that I had to do better, for her.

It seemed that Frost's words of encouragement were all I needed to get my head on right, they had also managed to line up with Hank's perfectly. They were both right, I needed to relax and when I returned for round three with Kyle I was focused and ready. I managed to hold out for over half an hour before he pinned me then we took a break for some much-needed food. With the rest and sustenance, and another confidence building talk from my sweetie, I was back in the clearing in wolf form an hour after we ate, ready to face Kyle again. This time I held him off, matched him move for move and then finally, almost twenty-five minutes in, got the upper hand. I pinned him and held him down, his scruff in my jaws and a look of defeat on his canine features that made me a bit giddy, not that I showed it right away. Once I let him up I pranced back over to Frost and pounced on her, bowling us both over a couple times and leaving her giggling as she ruffled my fur. "Good job baby! I knew you could do it!" I nuzzled her for a few moments and then shifted back and slipped into my clothes as Kyle crossed the clearing and chuckled a little.

"Well done girl. I'm impressed, but now the hard part starts. Barkley won't go down nearly as easily as the three of us did. You have your work cut out for you."

I knew he was right and I nodded that I understood that I was about to go through the training of my life. I would be working harder than I had ever worked on anything and for a moment I wondered what would happen if my training worked and I defeated Cameron on a challenge. I pushed the thought aside, deciding that I had plenty of time to ask that question later on and it could wait. Barkley told me that I would spend a few days working with Kyle, learning the finer points of staying focused and not letting my temper get the better of me. Each day he would give it a little more, hold back a little less and things would get very violent very quickly.

I thought I was ready but nothing could have prepared me for the ten days that followed training with the larger wolf. I spent my nights sore, battered, bruised and feeling like I could sleep for a month, but thankfully my mate was understanding, gentle and caring and looked after me. She handled my bursts of temper gracefully, massaged out the knots and kinks in my muscles and helped ice my bruises until they faded. She even helped stop the bleeding after a particularly nasty round with the bigger wolf left a massive bite in my left side that bled for over an hour. After ten days we had finally reached a point where, even when Kyle managed to get a few scratches or bites in, he could no longer pin me. Two days of being unable to pin me down and Barkley decided that I was ready to move on, ready to face him.

I was all at once excited and terrified for my first day of sparring with the Alpha, knowing that this would be more difficult than the other three combined and also knowing what was waiting for me after him. It was with my nerves on edge that I entered the clearing on our fourteenth day with the Sunshine pack and faced Barkley. He stripped and shifted, the change more seamless than any I had ever seen and I watched the huge pale blond wolf stretch himself in front of me and started to panic a little. He was almost twice my size and I didn't know how I was supposed to get the upper hand on him in any way. Not to mention the fact that even if I did, well, if he was this big, I could only imagine how massive Hank must be. That scared me and I wasn't too proud to admit it, at least not to myself, Frost and Abbey since they would both be able to see it anyway.

***

"You ready honey?" I glanced at Hank when he spoke and I knew when he chuckled that my face showed him exactly how not ready for this I actually was. "Look, don't panic lass. Just remember, no opponent is beyond you, just find their weakness. Bigger isn't always better, just different. You can do this, just know your opponent. Now go on."

He urged me into the clearing further and I managed to get out of my clothes and shift without shaking too much. I knew this would take a while to master, Kyle had taken me ten days, I could imagine that Barkley would take me weeks and Hank possibly months. I was prepared to at least try though, all I had was time and I would take as long as I needed to make sure that I was the one that walked away when I challenged Cameron. I planted my paws in the slightly damp earth, lowered my head and let my ears tilt forward as my eyes focused on my opponent across the clearing.

I had learned better than to make the first move, I was smaller, quicker, more agile but if they managed to get the first blow, that didn't matter and my advantage was lost. As it turned out a few moments later when Barkley came at me, he wasn't exactly heavy on his paws and was almost as agile as I was. That was a shock and it caught me off-guard which gave him the opening he needed. It only took him three minutes to have me pinned that first round and I had to admit that it beat my ego and pride down a few notches. I was embarrassed, but I had to pull myself up and try again, and again, and again as it turned out. Days passed and I was still attempting to get the upper hand with the Alpha, it wasn't going well at all and I was running out of tricks. I finally gave up trying tricks and just tried to outwit him, just my luck he was damn smart as well and it was easier said than done. Even after days of searching for any weakness in the Alpha I was still drawing blanks, and losing horribly.

CHAPTER TWELVE

MY BREAK came the day when I caught a chink in the big male's armor as it were and knew I'd found what I needed to beat him, I just had to figure out how to use it to my advantage. It seemed that the big Alpha was a little slow turning to his right and his reach that way wasn't what it was to the left. I started practicing dodging against my usual movements, knowing that the move would have to come naturally and be fluid to not be broadcast for him to see. After almost three weeks of working myself to the point that the new dodge and a few twists and attacks were coming naturally, I was ready to try them. I met Barkley in the clearing and prepared for our first round, considering whether or not to let him have a couple so I could warm up before I sprang my new training on him. That sounded good to me since I was still half asleep and I didn't try anything new the first two rounds, still holding out longer than I had those first couple days, but eventually ending up pinned.

On the third round I took my stand on my side of the clearing and waited, staring him down, letting him make the first move. He did and I waited for him to get close, faked a dodge and then slipped to his right and ripped into his shoulder as he went by. He let out a howl of pain and came skidding to a halt, looking at his shoulder in a bit of shock before he turned on me once more. He knew that I had found his weakness and he had to try and make up for it, something that he obviously thought he could do without much work. As it turned out, I managed to get the upper hand a few more times and by the time the round ended, I had not only made him bleed in a few places but had him pinned as well. I was proud of myself but not feeling the cocky self-confidence that I had exhibited after defeating Kyle. The celebration was a bit more reserved this time and while I was thrilled and definitely proud of what I had managed, I wasn't being a brat about it.

"Good job!"

Barkley's voice boomed from behind me as I tugged my right shoe back on, stood and turned only to be wrapped in a big bear hug. He was laughing and so was Hank, both apparently proud of the progress I had made over the few weeks I had been with them. I hugged him back and then received the same from Hank before being pounced on by Frost with an excited squeal. I giggled and hugged her tight then hugged Abbey as well, glad to see them both grinning from ear to ear about my accomplishment.

"Don't get too excited. I have to take on Hank next, he's gonna murder me!"

I laughed and that set everyone else off as well. Frost settled her arm around my waist and I leaned my head on her shoulder, happier in the last few weeks than I could ever remember being, even knowing what was waiting for me when I left Sunshine pack territory.

"Well we have faith in you."

My mate's confidence in me always made my heart warm and as she gave me a squeeze, I tilted my face up and kissed her neck. She shivered a little and smiled down at me with a little wink and I just smiled back up at her, glad that we'd had this time together, it had been so nice. We made our way back to the vehicles and then back into the housing area, setting up in the meeting hall Barkley and Hank had built years back for the pack to use for gatherings. The smell of food was already hanging in the air and it was wonderful, reminding me that I was starving. We took up our places with the Alphas, Faith, Justin, their kids and Kyle near the front of the room and waited for the food to be done. Within ten minutes the rest of the pack that wasn't involved in the cooking process began to enter the space and take up their places at tables.

Word of my final fight with Barkley had traveled through the pack and was the chatter of the first few minutes in the large space. I couldn't help but laugh a little at that, never having been the center of so much attention before and not sure what to do with it all. The food came out to the tables about the time everyone settled down to their usual places and the conversation paused long enough for everyone to fill up plates. Once everyone had a plate and was back in their seat, the chatting started up again and the topic at our table turned to serious matters.

"Alright, I've been putting this off because I knew I had time but, now that I'm about to start the final section I might as well ask. What happens after I challenge Cameron?" Barkley, Hank and Faith all exchanged looks with each other and even Frost looked like she knew something that she wasn't telling me.

"Well, then you take over the Rider pack." Frost had spoken but it took me a minute to register what she was telling me, and what exactly that meant.

"So I have to kill him then." She just nodded and I looked at Barkley then Hank and finally Faith and they each confirmed with their own nods. "Wow, okay. If that's the only way."

"It is, it's the only way to break the bond. Otherwise you'll still be linked to him and since that's exactly what you don't want, it's the only way out." I just nodded, I understood completely, no matter how sickening I found the whole deal, I had no choice.

"And you think that the pack will just let me take over as Alpha? Without a fight? Because I don't really see that happening." Frost shook her head a little and then turned her chair so she was facing me and drew in a deep but very unsteady breath.

"No, they won't like it but they won't have any choice. Once you kill Cameron you earn the right to lead the pack."

"Unless..." I turned my attention toward Barkley as Frost did the same, Hank was sitting beside his mate with his eyes glued to his plate and that couldn't mean anything good.

"Unless what?"

"Unless your father decides to challenge you for them. He's the strongest Alpha in the area and has the right to do just that."

"Perfect."

I growled the word under my breath and then huffed a little and realized that I was suddenly no longer hungry. I shoved my plate away, pushed my chair back and stood up, brushing my hand across Frost's shoulders as I left the table without saying another word. I made my way outside into the bite of the early January air and shivered from something other than the cold. I looked up into the rapidly rising moon and fought to keep from crying, not ready to give into possibly having to kill my own father. I felt the urge to run, so I did, I gave in and took off into the woods, not caring which way I was heading and not worrying about getting lost. I had an amazing sense of direction, we all did, even better in wolf form, and I would be able to find my way back no matter how far I went.

I stayed in human form, needing the sting of the cold air in my lungs and on my skin to keep me from losing it completely and giving into my emotions. I ran until my legs were sore and my lungs ached and then I stopped, dropped to my knees and gave into everything that I had been holding in. The pain, the anger, the sadness, the hurt, all of it came spilling out in a flood of warm tears that left salty streaks down my cheeks. I was lost in my sobs, face in my hands when I felt a wet nose on my neck and heard a familiar whimper. I wiped my eyes and looked over at my white wolf, not really even shocked that she had followed me and I just hugged her. She hooked one somehow dainty-despite-its-size paw around me and hugged me back as well as a wolf really could.

"It's all just too much, Frost." I couldn't handle everything that was being heaped on me, it was a lot for my system to take on its own and I was losing the battle with my emotional and mental states.

She couldn't speak to me but one look into those pale eyes, those purple irises shining back at me and I knew I wasn't alone, I had been insane to think I was for even a moment. I had support, people who loved me and who would give everything for me, I knew Frost would readily die for me, just like I would for her.

"It's not too much is it?" She gave me a fake sneeze and shook her head at me and I laughed a little at her very canine antics then scratched under her chin. "We'll just take this a step at a time and not let me get ahead of myself. Deal with Cam first, then we'll see what happens." She gave me a very exaggerated nod and I kissed her right between her eyes then nuzzled her before I kissed her nose. "Come on, let's get back."

We turned and made our way back through the woods and to the house we were borrowing, slipping inside and finding Abbey sitting in front of the fireplace.

"Are you okay?" She seemed a little frantic as she dropped the poker she'd been using to move logs around in the fire and rushed over to me. Frost slipped upstairs to the bedroom we'd been sharing for the last few weeks and shifted back, getting back into her clothes and then rejoined us as I calmed Abbey down.

"Abbey, I'm okay, really. I had a momentary freak out, ran into the woods, cried it out and I'm fine now. Thanks to Frost." I looked over my shoulder at my mate with a smile as she slipped her arms around me and kissed my temple.

"Well thank goodness. I was worried sick! I'm glad you're okay though, thanks for going after her Frost."

"Always."

That single word was the only response from my mate, and the only one that I needed to hear, the only one that meant anything just then. She would always come after me, always find me, always protect me, always bring me back and I had no doubt about that. We chatted in front of the fire until it burned down into barely more than embers and then slipped off into our bedrooms to get some sleep. Barkley wanted to give me a week or so to recover and enjoy myself before we started throwing me into the clearing with Hank. I was thankful for that and was looking forward to the rest and the chance to just relax and spend my days with Frost and Abbey rather than getting my butt handed to me.

CHAPTER THIRTEEN

I GOT my week off as promised, but then the training began again and it was brutal since Hank was exactly as massive as I had expected him to be. I was stuck fighting with a horse-sized wolf that was as solid as a brick wall and about as giving. I had been at it with the huge bulk of werewolf for almost two months and I was losing hope that I would ever manage to get the upper hand with him. He didn't seem to have a weakness, no soft spot, no impairments to take advantage of and it was getting me down. Not to mention the fact that my eighteenth birthday was rapidly approaching and I was more and more aware of the fact that all three of us, myself, Frost and Abbey, had completely missed the last of our senior year of high school. So much for making something of myself and getting somewhere in this world, once again, being a wolf had gotten in the way.

March flew by faster than I expected and before I knew it April was on us and I was still no closer to beating Hank. The man was impossible to defeat and I had started to lose any hope of managing to get through him. I woke the morning of April thirteenth to Frost nuzzling my neck and just smiled as I snuggled back against her, the only indication I was even awake. "Happy birthday baby." I yawned and opened my eyes as I turned over so I could get my arms around my mate, wishing that we'd had the chance to wake up together like this for her eighteenth.

"Thank you love." She kissed me and I kissed her back, still not tired of waking up beside her and honestly not thinking I would ever get tired of it. I stretched and then rolled to the other side of the bed and slipped out of it, knowing that, birthday or not, I had a full day of fighting ahead of me. Something about it being my birthday made me feel like I could do anything, like I just might have a chance at getting through this with Hank. I rushed through a shower, dressed and then headed downstairs to chat with Abbey while Frost cleaned up. I knew she hadn't been ready for me to leave the bed but I had to get through this training, get past Hank or we would be hiding here in California forever. I was ready to go home, ready to deal with Cameron and ready to take Frost as my mate for real, by pack law.

I made my way to the truck with Abbey. Moments later Frost joined us and we made our way to the clearing. The Sunshine pack had arranged breakfast pack cookout style for my birthday and I was thrilled at the idea. Most of the pack was already there when we arrived and a few of the wolves cheered and most wished me a happy birthday as we crossed to our usual cookout table. We were just settling in when Heath, one of the pack Omegas, rushed into the clearing and came skidding to a halt next to our table out of breath.

"Heath! What's going on? What's got you so worked up?"

"Wolves Barkley, ones I don't recognize and a lot of them!"

Barkley exchanged a look with Hank and they were on their feet in seconds without so much as a word. Faith, Justin, Frost, Abbey and I were right behind them and the small group was starting across the clearing when the wolves Heath spoke of burst from the woods across from us. I stopped dead in my tracks and narrowed my eyes at them, a few of them looked a little more familiar than I liked. A figure stepped out of the trees behind the wolves, a very human figure and a gasp ripped from me then another from Frost and I grabbed for her hand.

"He wouldn't dare." Frost's voice was shaky as she spoke and I looked over at her as I squeezed her hand and she leaned against me.

"Yeah baby, he would." Barkley and Hank glanced at me and I held each of their gazes for a few moments and then turned my attention back to the male now crossing the clearing toward us. "You shouldn't be here. You have no right to be on this land."

"I have every right, Kyndle. My mate has been hiding here against my wishes, being harbored by another pack. It's about time I teach them, and you, a lesson." I narrowed my eyes at him and growled and he just laughed at me a little and shook his head, far too full of himself.

"I take it you're Cameron?" Hanks question was barely a question at all given my reaction and when Cameron turned toward the massive Alpha, I saw his confidence falter just slightly and it made me smirk a little.

"I am. Not that it's any of your business." He had recovered quickly and snapped his retort back at the bigger male. I never had thought he was very smart, but now I had living proof of it.

"It is my business when you bring your wolves onto my land and around my pack without being invited or even announcing your presence. Bad politics, little Alpha." I watched Cameron sneer at the larger man's choice of words and had to bite back a laugh at him being called 'little Alpha', it made my day.

"Our business here has nothing to do with you. We don't want any trouble; I just want my mate. She's eighteen now and I intend to take the next step of our bonding. You won't stand in my way." Hank and Barkley both narrowed their eyes at him but then they stepped aside and Barkley raised an eyebrow at him.

"By all means, take her... If you can." He grinned at me

with those last three words and I turned and flashed Cameron the most wicked smile I could manage.

"*IF* I can? Excuse me? And who exactly is going to stop me?"

"I am."

The words came out steady and without even a hint of fear or hesitation and despite the fact that Hank had been kicking my furry behind up and down the clearing for weeks I actually felt ready to take Cameron on. He laughed at me, outright, not even pretending to try and hold it back and I prickled a little bit at the reaction, but held it back.

"Really? You think you'll stop me from taking you back?"

"I do. Cameron... I challenge you."

That cut his laughter off immediately and he looked at me with rage behind his eyes. His expression said he was ready to rush me right that moment. I didn't flinch, I wasn't scared of him anymore, he held no power over me and I knew in that moment that only one of us would be walking out of that clearing. It would be me, hell itself opening up around me wouldn't stop me from kicking his ass.

"Challenge me? An Alpha's challenge?" I nodded in agreement with his assessment and he snorted a little and then shook his head at me as if I'd lost my mind. "Are you serious little girl? You really think to challenge me?" I just quirked one brow at him and he started laughing again, obviously thinking that I'd managed to lose my mind in California.

"Unless you're scared. Afraid you'll lose, Cameron?"

That shut him up, fast, and he stood there and glared at me, a growl dripping from him as he flashed teeth my way. He was losing his control and I was fine with that; I actually smiled a little as I cocked my head a bit and watched him, waiting.

"I fear nothing girl. Let's do this, but when I best you, you will come back home with me and finish this bonding."

"No." That stopped him and made him turn that glare on me yet again, he really wasn't used to hearing the word no and it shocked him.

"Excuse me?"

"You heard me. You'll have to kill me, because I'll never stop fighting you. And I intend to kill you, Cameron, to be rid of you for good."

That sent him into a rage and he came at me across the clearing, the knife he carried on his belt glinting in his hand. In that moment, I was scared for the first time as my mind flashed back to the dream I'd had that night so many weeks ago. Barkley stopped him and twisted the knife from his hand before he had even made it within thirty feet of me.

"You've been challenged and you will do this right, with honor. Give her less than the respect she deserves as another Alpha and expect this pack to turn on you for your dirty tricks. Understood?"

Cameron seemed to sober a little at the words and nodded to the larger Alpha then turned back to slip out of his clothes. I turned to Frost, slipped out of my clothes, and handed them to her, and then pulled her in and kissed her, lingering as long as I dared. The growl I heard from behind me let me know that Cameron had not only shifted but had seen me kiss his sister. It pissed him off and I didn't care, let him be pissed, it would make him emotional and predictable, easy to beat. I shifted and my paws were barely on the ground before he launched himself at me, covering the ground of the clearing fast. Thankfully I was quick back to my senses after so much time shifting to fight and I easily sidestepped him.

He breezed by me and then slid to a stop, kicking up earth and debris as he did so and then turned on me again. His anger flashed in his eyes as he charged at me, he took a leap at me and at the last moment I ducked, cradling myself against the dirt and letting him sail over me. I tipped my muzzle up as he went over and heard a howl of pain as my teeth caught his sensitive belly and ripped a few bloody lines into it. He landed hard, lost his paws and rolled a few times as I regained my legs and whipped around to charge him while he was down. He had just managed to pull himself onto his paws and was still shaking a bit when I lowered my head a barreled headlong into his side. I heard the sickening crunch of ribs breaking and hopped over him when he hit the ground, moving a few yards away to wait and see if he got up.

He was on his feet again a few moments later and I lowered my head to wait for his next move, feeling like I had the upper hand already. Unfortunately, I let myself get a little bit cocky and that led to being a split second late in reaction when he moved again. I felt him hit me in the chest and I was thrown backwards into the dirt, my head contacting a rock and leaving me stunned for a few moments. It was just long enough and he lunged at me, catching my left shoulder in his jaws and biting down hard. I yelped in pain as teeth met bone and knew he had at the very least damaged the muscles in my left shoulder if not severed them completely. I got my back legs under him and kicked him off of me then pulled myself up onto my three good legs, the left front one almost useless until I could shift to start the process of healing it. I turned on him as he rushed me again and lost my balance as he hit me, knocking me off my feet and onto my side, my torn shoulder in the dirt.

I let out a howl as pain ripped through me and saw stars for a moment until the shock of it subsided, then I pulled myself up again. This was getting bad fast and I had to do something to regain some ground in this fight, it couldn't end this way. Before I could come up with anything, he was on me again, I hadn't even seen him coming this time and he had me pinned on my back, his jaws around my throat. So this was how it was going to end for me, at the jaws of the mate I'd had forced onto me by my father while the woman I loved watched. The most pathetic whimper that ever left any living creature slipped out of me as I thought of never seeing Frost again, never holding her, never kissing her. The noise caused Cameron to falter for a second and I seized the moment as I felt his muscles relax to turn on him.

I twisted my neck from his jaws and used my good shoulder to shove him off of me which caught him just enough off guard to send him sprawling in the dirt. I pounced on him, grabbed the back of his neck between my teeth and heard him whine at me, knowing he was doing his best to plead for his life. I felt muscles begin to shift and rearrange and knew he was about to change back, not something I could let happen. Killing him was one thing, having to look into his human face as I did it was another and I just couldn't do it. I closed my eyes, steadied myself and clamped down hard, teeth digging into flesh, tearing through muscle and finally hitting bone. I forced myself to keep going and felt the crunch of bones snapping and crushing between my jaws, heard his strangled howl as he tried to get free and then silence.

I waited a few moments for the bleeding to stop, his severed jugular finishing the job quickly, and then I released him and let him drop to the dirt, limp. It was done, over, he was dead and I wondered if it had managed to sever the bond we had gone through. I was just about to shift back and ask when a sudden pain ripped through me, searing itself through my body and taking the choice of shifting from me. The change happened suddenly and without warning, leaving me writhing in pain and screaming as my shoulder attempted to knit back together. Frost was at my side in seconds but I barely registered her presence through the pain that was wracking my body. At some point I heard a voice telling me to relax and just let it happen, but I was having trouble understanding what whoever it was meant by that.

The pain finally eased off, an ache in its wake that throbbed through me and left me shivering and twitching. I had almost blacked out at least twice during the last several minutes and my shoulder felt like it was on fire, but I was awake and I was alive. Alive. That was the one that mattered the most in that moment and I finally got my wits about me enough to sit up and find Frost. She was sitting beside me in tears and looking like she wanted to hold me, but was terrified to touch me. I reached for her with my right arm, still not trusting that my left would work properly and she wrapped her arms around me and buried her face against the front of my right shoulder.

"Shhhh, I'm okay love. I'm alive, I'm alive." She just nodded against my shoulder a few times and then leaned back and smiled at me, the tears still falling but seeming to do so out of happiness rather than pain or fear now.

"I know, and you severed the bond." I glanced to Barkley and Hank and they both nodded to confirm that Frost was right, the bond had been broken, I was free of Cameron for good.

"Was that what hurt so bad?"

"Partly. Severing a bond does hurt, but what you felt was trying to heal a major injury after severing that bond. Your healing process had been pulling energy from Cameron the last several weeks while we'd been beating the crap out of you. Your body got used to it and then with this injury tried it again and when he wasn't there, well, it hurt more." I could agree with that, it had hurt like hell and it still ached like it wouldn't heal completely for weeks or longer.

"Well, at least it's over. I have a question."

"Shoot kiddo." Hank was smiling at me, obviously proud of what I had managed despite how close I had come to losing my life in the process.

"The bonding, do the Elders have to be present and performing it?"

"Not at all. As a matter of fact, any Alpha can perform the initial bonding. Why?" He grinned at me as if he knew what was coming but wanted me to say it anyway and I just smiled and looked at Frost.

"Frost, you can finally be my mate. For real. Will you? We can do it tonight, before we have to go back and deal with the pack and all the politics. What do you say?" She let out a little laugh that more than told me she thought I sounded silly for even thinking I needed to ask and just leaned over and kissed me.

"You know the answer to that, Kyndle. And if you don't you need your head examined. I've wanted to be your mate for two years. Yes, baby, of course I will."

I kissed her again and then hugged her as well as I could

with one shoulder injured before I let her lean away and get to her feet. She helped me up and I hugged Abbey and then Barkley, Hank, Faith and Justin in turn and got a high five from Kyle which made me laugh. We cleaned up the mess Cameron and I had made in the clearing while Heath, Kyle, Justin and several of the other males removed Cameron's body and dealt with it. Dirt was kicked over the bloody spots in the clearing to cover them up and the cooking resumed as did the chatter. It was nice to watch things return to normal and as I glanced around, I didn't see any of the offending Rider wolves anywhere. If I knew them they had cleared out to tell my father what had happened the moment I had killed Cameron.

I pushed all that aside, I wasn't dealing with it today, it was my birthday, I was free of Cameron and would be bonded to Frost as soon as the moon was up. It had to be the best birthday I'd ever had, almost being killed withheld of course, and I planned on making the most of the rest of it. After we ate, Frost and I went for a walk through the woods, knowing that we were completely free of any lurking danger now. It was nice to just walk, not having anywhere to go or anything on the agenda, just for the sheer pleasure of it. We wasted so much time that it was getting dark by the time we returned to the clearing and we were more than ready for the bonding ceremony. It had been two years in the making and we had started to believe that it would never actually happen so the fact that it was about to was making us both shiver a bit with excitement.

CHAPTER FOURTEEN

WE STEPPED up to Barkley and Hank and they had us face each other as the moon rose overhead, it was full and looked amazing as the sun retreated below the horizon, painting the sky around it in pinks, purples and oranges. They gave us the words, we repeated them and in a matter of minutes we were bound and I felt a rush of energy breeze through me. I gasped and looked at Frost who smiled at me to show that she had felt it too and we both looked at the males who had just helped us seal our love.

"That's the bond."

"But it didn't do that with Cameron."

"It wouldn't have, you were forced into that. This is what the bond feels like when you're bound to someone you love."

Frost and I looked at each other for a moment and then I tugged her closer, wrapped my arms around her neck and kissed her. She returned the gesture with everything she had in her and we stayed there for a few long minutes, just letting the last lingering bits of sunlight haze leave the horizon before we parted. I raised an eyebrow at her and she laughed a little and then nodded and we dropped each other's hands, stripped off our clothes and took off across the clearing. We both shifted as we hit the tree line and then I was running beside my white wolf, my beautiful mate, the woman that I would spend the rest of eternity with.

We ran until we couldn't run anymore, joined by Abbey and the members of the Sunshine pack at some point. When we finally slowed, we turned, nuzzled each other and then made our way back toward the clearing. After shifting back and getting back into our clothes, we waited for Abbey who changed, dressed and then pulled Faith aside and spoke with her for a moment. She finally nodded and hugged the other woman, then her mate and joined us at the truck so we could head back to the house. I didn't ask her what she'd been talking to Faith about, she would tell me when, and if, she was ready. We pulled up to the house and when Frost and I moved to get out of the truck Abbey didn't turn it off and I gave her a look. "I'm gonna stay with Faith and Justin tonight. You guys need some time alone. I'll see you in the morning. Night!"

With that she pulled away and left me standing there grinning and shaking my head, that was my best friend, always a step ahead. I turned to Frost and she winked at me, sending a little flutter through my stomach as I registered what had just happened. I was eighteen, we were just bonded as mates and Abbey had given us the night alone together after waiting for almost three years. My mouth went dry and I was suddenly nervous as hell to go into that house with my new mate, not actually sure what to do. She seemed to sense my hesitation and stepped over to me, wrapping her arms around my waist and just looked at me.

"Calm down love. It's not that scary, we've been skirting this situation for almost three years. Don't you think it's about time we just... Do it?"

I nodded slowly, she was right of course, there was no reason to keep putting it off now, not after we'd already been through the first step of bonding. She gave a nod toward the house, slipped her hands into mine and started up the steps then slowly across the porch and through the front door. She kicked it closed and led me up the stairs into the master bedroom, kicking that door closed too.

"Hey, relax a little, okay? We don't have to do anything, I understand if you still aren't ready." That brought me back to myself, how could I not be ready to be with her? Hell, I had been ready on some level or another since we were freshman and I knew that it was just nerves.

"No, I don't want to wait, Frost. I want this, I want you. I always have. I'm just..."

"Nervous?"

"Yeah..." She gave me a small smile and stepped over close, pressing herself against me as she leaned her lips close to my ear and whispered to me.

"Me too."

I was shocked, she sure didn't seem very nervous, at least not nearly as nervous as I was letting myself be. I looked at her and she nodded a little then her cheeks flushed pink and I couldn't help but smile and pull her lips to mine, I loved it when she blushed. Words were lost when our lips met, our first private kiss since the bonding and it only took a few moments for it to grow into something much more passionate than either of us had ever allowed. We had spent so long being careful, not crossing that line, knowing that neither of us was ready. We'd also known that it would make things even more difficult if the time ever came that we had to be separated.

Now that we were letting it go, it felt amazing. My arms wrapped around her neck as hers found my waist and I practically melted into her, not knowing how I had managed to make it so long without feeling like this with her. My senses were thrown into overdrive when I felt her hands slip under my shirt, my skin tingling where her fingertips brushed over it. I let her explore for a few moments, not really wanting to break the kiss to allow my shirt to be removed, but then I just needed it gone. I pulled away and leaned back, helping her pull the tank top over my head and then mirrored the movement with her shirt. We left them both on the floor where they landed and my more dominant personality finally kicked in.

I led her over to the bed we had been sharing, but behaving ourselves in for almost six months and I backed her onto it. Once she was sitting, I looked down at her, running my fingers through her pale hair like I had so many times before. It was so much more this time and it all at once made all the sense in the world and absolutely no sense at all. I bent down and kissed her again as I worked the hooks on her bra loose and helped her out of that piece of clothing as well. She removed mine and I eased her back further onto the bed, crawling up onto it over her and laying her back, never losing her lips as my hands roamed her naked upper body. I tickled and teased my way down her chest and stomach and then worked the button and zipper on her jeans open.

I made quick work of them, taking her underwear with them and then I pulled my knees up either side of hers and pulled away from her lips finally, sitting up and pulling my hair over one shoulder so I could look down at her. The sight of her laying completely bare underneath me took my breath away and I couldn't look away. She was stunning and I had to remind myself that she was mine, that all of that pale, toned and perfect body was mine forever. Her cheeks tinted pale red as she looked up at me and I smiled at her as I leaned down and kissed the little hollow where her neck met her collarbone.

"Gods you're beautiful."

I felt her entire body heat and knew she would be in full blush in a matter of moments, but I didn't bother to look for it. I moved back to her lips, claiming them and not feeling the least bit timid or nervous any longer, just wanting my mate. She seemed to take a few moments to get her limbs working and then went right for the waistband of my jeans, working my button and zipper as easily as I had hers. I helped her get the offending denim off, as well as my underwear and then finally pressed myself down onto her. The entire length of my body against hers, skin on skin and the sensation made us both shiver as I heard a whimper escape her. The sound made my heart skip a little and my breathing pick up and without pulling away from her lips I shifted my weight to one side a bit and let my hand drift down her bare skin.

My weight was rested on my good right shoulder and I just hoped that my left would hold out enough to do what I wanted to do. I needed her tonight, I was done waiting and I had the feeling that she was right there with me on the matter. Her breath hitched here and there as my fingertips brushed over sensitive areas and I memorized them as I moved lower, tracing every inch of bare skin I could find. I finally broke from the kiss so I could follow my fingertips with my lips, needing more of her every second that passed. My lips skimmed lightly down her neck as my fingers traced down her stomach and around her belly button, making the muscles twitch and flutter with the contact.

My lips found her right nipple just as my fingers dipped over her hip and trailed down her right thigh, my touch feather-light. She gasped as my tongue grazed her nipple and then shuddered when I wrapped my lips around it and pulled it into my mouth. A whimper slipped from her when I nipped at the rapidly-hardening little peak lightly and that whimper turned into a breathy moan as one fingertip dipped between her lips and found her clit. I eased around it in slow circles as I swapped over to her left nipple and I felt her breath catch and then release in a ragged sigh. I worked circles over the sensitive spot for a few moments and then my finger and my lips moved down together. My finger edged around her opening, already wet and waiting as my lips continued down her body. I flicked my tongue into her belly button and she squirmed a little under me, whining softly as I teased her with tongue and fingers.

She rolled her hips against me and I raised an eyebrow at how eager she was being, unable to make her wait anymore. I eased a finger inside her as my tongue met the clit that same finger had abandoned only moments earlier. The moan that was ripped from my mate made my eyelids flutter a little and left heat pooling low in my belly. Gods how I loved the way that sounded and I couldn't wait to hear more of it. I eased my finger out and worked two back in slowly, not wanting to hurt her, but she responded by gasping out my name and grabbing a handful of my hair. Tongue and fingers began working together, finding a rhythm that made Frost writhe and pant as she rolled and bucked against me. Whatever inhibitions she might have had before were completely melted away as she responded to the things I was doing to her body.

I was intent on staying the course until I had her screaming but after a minute or so she dragged my mouth from her and pulled me back up her body. She allowed my fingers to stay in place and I held the rhythm I had started as she pulled me in and kissed me, her tongue exploring my mouth like never before. She was still kissing me when I felt her hand working down my body and knew what she was up to. I definitely wasn't about to stop her. We parted after a few moments and she watched my face as her fingers did what mine had done a short time earlier. The moment I felt the contact my eyes slipped closed and my head fell forward against her shoulder as I whimpered her name. It wasn't long before she was inside me and we had found a rhythm that had us both breathing hard and on the edge. I took that last step and curled my fingers up, hitting that sensitive spot just inside her as my thumb found her clit and started massaging it.

She followed the move a moment later and in seconds I felt her body tense under me, her walls clamped down around my fingers and her back arched up against me as she screamed my name. She stifled the sound by biting my shoulder, the sting of her teeth breaking the skin sending me over the edge. The climax rocked me so hard that I couldn't breathe for a moment and then sparks exploded behind my eyelids and I cried out against her shoulder. She urged me toward the base of her neck and I bit down hard, tasting her blood on my tongue as we both began to come down. My pulse was racing, my breathing ragged and my muscles felt like I'd just run a double marathon. It was amazing. I laid there for a few moments until I felt her tongue flick over the bite on my shoulder and I turned and did the same to hers. I rolled off to the side so she could catch her breath without my weight on top of her, but then snuggled right up against her side.

"Wow," she said to the ceiling, her voice barely more than a whisper and her heart still pounding against her ribcage under my hand.

"Mmhmm. Wow." Was all I could manage in response, figuring that we had said it all already and nothing more needed to be spoken about it.

CHAPTER FIFTEEN

WE SPENT the rest of the night exploring and getting to know one another in ways we never had before, finally falling asleep wrapped up together around four in the morning. I woke in a tangle of arms and legs, the golden rays of the afternoon sun warming the room and casting a few shadows on the walls. I was in heaven and I couldn't imagine that anything could ever make me feel better than I did just then. I nuzzled closer against Frost's side, my face buried in her neck and I felt her arms tighten around me and knew she'd been awake before me.

"Good morning my love." I smiled at the sexy morning rasp in her voice and nuzzled my way up her neck so I could kiss her chin.

"Mmmm, morning baby."

I knew we needed to get moving, we had a long drive ahead of us to get back into Rider territory and as much as we didn't want to deal with the fallout of Cameron's death, I had to go take my new place. I grumbled a little and rolled away from my mate with a yawn then winced a bit and reached up to touch the bite on my shoulder. I looked over and caught sight of the matching bite on Frost and just grinned a little, we had marked each other.

"Well, looks like we completed the full bonding circle." She looked at me a little confused and I reached out and brushed my fingertips over the already-healing bite on her pale skin. She gasped a little as she touched it and saw mine at the same time then blushed a deep crimson and I couldn't help but laugh.

"I'm sorry, I hope I didn't hurt you."

The shyness that had crept into her voice seemed almost ludicrous given the things we had done the night before, and that morning, but it was adorable. I reached over and hooked my hand behind her neck, drawing her over closer to me and kissed the tip of her nose.

"Not at all. Come on, we need to get moving. As much as I would love nothing more than to stay in bed with you all day, it'll have to wait until we go play politics."

She growled at the thought of dealing with her older, and now brand new, pack and I couldn't help but agree with her. It couldn't be avoided forever though, and all that we would accomplish by staying away would be to throw the pack into chaos and we couldn't have that. She huffed and pushed away from me then rolled out of the bed to get herself ready for the day and I followed her. As much of a rush as we may be in, we still managed to take the time to get reacquainted in the shower, probably taking longer than we should have, but I deemed it necessary. We had only been mated for a few hours after all, who could really blame us for wanting to get every moment we could together before returning to reality.

Once we were dried and dressed, we packed our things, and Abbey's, then headed for the door and I laughed a little when I saw the stylish scarf that Frost was wearing. I shook my head and pulled it from her neck, revealing the bite mark that I knew she was trying to hide.

"Don't cover it up baby. We have nothing to hide anymore. Wear it proudly, like I will."

I glanced down at my shoulder where she had bitten me the night before, the spot left completely open to view by the tank top I was wearing. She smiled at me, stuffed the scarf into her bag and then nodded and pulled the door open so we could meet the world together for the first time as an Alpha pair. We locked up the house and made our way toward Barkley and Hank's home, finding them outside with Faith, Justin and Abbey. They all waved and we waved back as we walked up and I handed Abbey her bag with a smile and she just smirked back at me.

"What?"

"Good night?"

She asked the question as she nodded toward the mark on my shoulder and then glanced over at the matching mark on Frost's neck and I just smiled at her. Frost was at least three shades of red and I couldn't help but laugh as I wrapped an arm around her and pulled her in against my side. I kissed her temple and she relaxed against me, the blush easing off a little bit as she leaned on me and we waited for Abbey to say her goodbyes. We stepped up to say goodbye to our new friends, agreeing to come back and visit eventually, but I realized that someone was missing.

"Where's Kyle?"

"He'll be along any minute, had a few things to tie up."

I looked at Barkley confused for a moment, what could the guy have to tie up that couldn't wait until after we'd gotten on the road? That question was answered when he appeared carrying a bag a few moments later, a bag that he promptly dropped when Abbey threw herself into his arms and he hugged her.

"I still can't believe you're coming with us!"

She was so excited that I had to do a double take for a moment before I realized what must be happening. I cleared my throat and Abbey turned toward the two of us, Frost looking just as shocked as I was, apparently she had missed the connection as well.

"Oh, um, okay so. While you were busy training and Frost was busy worrying about you, Kyle and I discovered that we have a lot in common and, well, he's coming back with us."

I turned toward Barkley and Hank, knowing that we needed them to be okay with losing a member of their pack to another or issues could arise.

"You two are alright with this?"

"Of course! Who are we to stand in the way of love?"

I glanced at Abbey when the word love hit the air and she just blushed a little and leaned closer into Kyle who looked down at her and smiled. It was true, I could see it written all over both of their faces, they were completely in love. How could I possibly argue with that?

"Okay! We're off then. Come on you two, let's get out of here."

We piled into the now very familiar truck, Abbey driving, Kyle beside her in the passenger seat and Frost and I cuddled together in the back. We had a long drive, but Abbey and Kyle had agreed to do all the driving, knowing that Frost and I would have a lot to deal with once we made it back to Rider pack territory. I wasn't looking forward to it and I knew that she wasn't either, after all, it was her brother that had been killed, by his mate, who was now her mate. This could get really messy and we both knew that we could end up in a fight for the pack, or with the pack. We slept on and off through the ride, awake long enough between naps to grill Abbey and Kyle about their new relationship and to talk about what we might encounter once we got home.

As it turned out, nothing could have really prepared us for what we came face to face with when we made it back to pack land. Abbey pulled up in front of Cameron's old house and I shivered as I remembered the events that had taken place the last time I'd been there. Frost sensed my unease and stayed close, keeping some form of contact with me the entire time we were near the house. We only stayed long enough to make sure that it was in one piece and then moved on into the meeting grounds, the clearing the pack used for official business. We knew that they were aware we had returned. We had seen scouts from both Rider and Clipper packs on the road approaching town. Both packs would be well informed of our return by now and I fully expected my father to try and interfere with the return. Frost and I stepped into the meeting grounds, Abbey and Kyle behind us and faced the very angry and confused-looking Rider pack.

The first to cross the clearing and approach us was Freddie, Cameron and Frost's uncle and the Rider pack Beta under Cameron. He didn't look happy and I knew that we would be in for a fight with this male. He had always believed he should have been Alpha, not Cameron. He would fight that point again now. Cameron had taken up his challenge, fought him and allowed him to live on and be Beta, I would allow no such mercy for the male. He was obstinate and insubordinate and if I was going to try and run this pack with Frost, we needed higher ranking members who would support us and have our backs, not be trying to tear us down at every turn. He stepped right up into my space, only a couple feet from me and definitely closer than I'd like, but I stood firm, not moving, not giving him the satisfaction of knowing how much I hated having him so close to me.

He raised a hand a swung at me and before I could even react his swing had been stopped mid-air and a threatening growl came from my right. I smiled a little, not needing to look to know that my mate had stopped that slap before it could get to me and was warning the male not to touch me.

"Lay a hand on her and I'll kill you myself Fredrick."

The words were tinged with a growl and sounded as angry as I'm sure the expression on her face was at that moment. I knew then what I had known since the day we first admitted our feelings for each other, she would never let anyone hurt me. I had my protector in Frost, who at first sight might seem the more delicate of the two of us, but she had a protective streak in her five miles wide. She wouldn't let this man, or anyone, hurt me if she had anything to say about it and now that she was my mate, she had everything to say about it.

He loosed a low growl in Frost's direction and that made me move, in seconds I had his wrist out of her grip and in mine and had twisted his arm around behind his back. He was easily five inches taller than me, but I was stronger, quite a bit so, and even as he tried to fight my grip, I tightened it and kicked the backs of his knees to drop him in front of me. The rest of the Rider pack had emerged into the clearing and had been watching the exchange from a safe distance. None of them looked happy.

"A few things need to change around here in the next few days. I'm sure you've all heard by now that Cameron is dead."

"Yes, thanks to this bitch we no longer have an Alpha!" Freddie had shouted the words toward the pack and a few growls erupted in the group as several members stepped forward.

"Shut up." I twisted his arm a bit harder and he yelped and looked down at the ground he was kneeling on, hopefully silenced. "It's true, I killed Cameron, I was left with no choice. However, you aren't without an Alpha. Unless you've all forgotten, he was attempting to force me into a bonding because I'm an Alpha."

"You have no rights over this pack! Freddie is next in the line!" This was shouted from somewhere in the middle of the crowd that was now pushing in closer toward us.

"He's right." Freddie chuckled and I just planted my foot in the middle of his back and kicked him over on his face in the dirt, I would deal with him later.

"Actually, I'm next in line." Frost's voice was strong and unwavering beside me and the murmur that swept the crowd made me grin a little. "With my brother dead, I have the right to take over this pack. However, I have no intention of doing so. I fully intend for my mate to do that..." She stepped over and slipped her arm around my waist and I smiled at her and wrapped mine back around her. "...and I believe she's ready to fill that void." I nodded to her to indicate that I was more than ready to step in and take over where her brother had left off, and hopefully do better than he had.

"I don't think so. It won't happen, not as long as I'm alive."

The voice came from behind us this time and I knew it

instantly, the familiar tone of it sending a shiver rippling through me. I reigned it in and turned to face the owner of the voice that had uttered the offending words.

"Father."

CHAPTER SIXTEEN

"KYNDLE. WHAT have you done?"

I simply shrugged since I figured what I had done was fairly obvious, I had done what I had to do to break myself free of the life he had tried to force on me against my will.

"My scouts told me you killed Cameron."

I just nodded, not seeing any reason to elaborate on the matter further, he had the bulk of it and that was what he needed to know.

"Well, I suppose maybe he wasn't a good enough male for you then. I should have known; he was so weak. We'll just have to find someone else, someone a bit more worthy, yes?" I snorted and shook my head. He obviously hadn't gotten all of the news or he would know that the suggestion was ridiculous. A wolf couldn't have more than one mate and I was bound, mind, body and soul to Frost, for the rest of time.

"Such a reaction, it isn't too late. You're only eighteen, we can find a good, strong male for you. A proper Alpha."

"No need old man. You're too late, I'm mated." I watched his eyes go wide and then, in typical Alpha male fashion, his gaze scanned the people I was with and settled on Kyle. He sniffed the air, no doubt catching the scent of Beta wolf all over the other male since that was exactly what he was, and growled at him. "Oh relax, that's Kyle, he's here with Abbey, not me. Though he is a nice guy. No, my mate is right here." I pulled Frost down and kissed her temple as she locked eyes with my father and refused to look away from the cycle of emotions that flickered through his eyes. First confusion, then irritation and finally a rage that settled behind his eyes and seared through the two of us.

"No, no, you couldn't have, it's not possible."

"We did and it's completely possible. And the bond is complete, you can't do a damn thing about it." I had to admit that as I watched the disbelief and then understanding flash through him, only to be replaced by that rage again, I felt a little smug and more than a bit proud of myself.

"Oh there is something I can do about it, I can kill your ridiculous little white wolf." His threat and the look he turned on Frost boiled my blood and I stepped between them with a growl, my hand planted in the middle of his chest.

"You won't touch her. The only right you have here is the right of challenge for the pack as another Alpha and that would be against me, not Frost. Challenge me if you want, but I won't let you lay a finger on her."

He was well aware of the truth behind my words and I also knew he could see that I knew what I was talking about in my eyes because he narrowed his own and took a couple steps back. I watched him think about his options for a moment, considering what to do before he raised an eyebrow and opened his mouth to speak, but I cut him off before he could utter a word.

"Before you challenge me Dane, know something... Don't start this if you can't finish it. You'll have to kill me, I won't give up my right to this pack while I'm alive, not to the likes of you."

It took him a moment, but he finally realized what I was saying, I was prepared to kill him if I had to, to protect myself and Frost. He had to be willing to do the same or he wouldn't survive long into a challenge and he knew that far too well. He shook his head, turned on his heel and walked away and I knew that, for the moment at least, he was letting the issue drop. He might change his mind down the line but for now he was letting me retain leadership of the Rider pack. Now it was just a matter of convincing the pack that being led by two eighteen-year-old girls wasn't the end of the world. The Riders were as traditional as the Clippers and I knew that we would have an uphill battle coming our way, most likely led by Fredrick. I turned my attention back to the male in question and eyed him warily, he needed to be dealt with, immediately. I thought for a moment and then turned back to Abbey and Kyle and waved them over to me so I could talk to them. We spoke for a few minutes, Abbey, Kyle, Frost and myself and then I turned and walked over to Freddie.

"Get up." I waited for him to get to his feet and then I looked him over and shook my head, actually rather disgusted with him. "I'm giving you one chance here. You step down as Beta willingly."

"What?!?!" He was obviously put out by the suggestion and didn't want to even consider it, but I stopped what he was about to say with a hand up in front of him.

"You step down willingly now or I'll take it as a challenge to my position and I'll kill you in a fight. Your choice."

"The pack can't function without a Beta." He was right of course, but I knew something that he didn't know and it would make him obsolete in the pack.

"I have a Beta. Abbey." She stepped up just behind my right shoulder when I spoke her name and stared the bigger man down. He sputtered a little, but then grumbled, let out a little frustrated growl and stepped back from the four of us to rejoin the rest of the pack.

"Fine... But don't think you've heard the last from me."

"Of course I haven't, but we'll be ready."

I had no doubt that those words were true, just like I had no doubt that, at some point, I would end up having to kill Fredrick. He was a threat to the pack, to me, to Frost and to everything that I was hoping to do with these wolves and I would eventually have to deal with that.

"Listen everyone. I'm not asking you to just immediately be okay with this change in leadership, I know it's sudden and it will be tough on you all, but it's happening all the same. I won the right to lead this pack fairly through a challenge and I intend to do the best I can to be fair to you all. I am not Cameron, or his father and I don't intend to rule you with fear and pain and threats, I intend to lead with kindness, fairness and understanding. Those who think I can't do it, or just don't want me to, are free to leave, I'll give you the month to decide where you stand with the pack. If you wish to leave, let me know and I'll release you with my blessing. For those who stay, there's a long road ahead, but I think we can make it work."

I firmly believed everything that I had just said and I knew that with Frost and Abbey at my side I could handle whatever this pack threw at me. I watched as the pack dispersed from the clearing and let out a sigh of relief that no one had outright spoken up against us other than Freddie. I could handle him, I wasn't sure I could handle a dozen or more angry Omegas, that was just a recipe for disaster. I leaned back against Frost when I felt her arms around me, suddenly very tired, but also very aware that I had no clue where we were going to be living. I turned around in her arms and caught her eyes and she seemed to read my mind because she gave me a little nod and started leading me back toward the mass of houses the pack lived in. We passed the house Cameron had lived in and she hugged me closer, knowing what I had been through in that place several months earlier.

"Here." She stepped onto the porch of one of the houses that looked like it hadn't been lived in for years and I just looked at it confused. "It belonged to my grandparents. Been empty since I was six. They wanted me to have it someday so, here we are." She unlocked the door as I smiled at her and then we stepped inside and I was immediately hit with a sense of ease, a feel of home. "You're a lot like my grandma, she always said she didn't know why her daughter ended up with my father. He was mean, downright cruel even and it tore grandma up to watch him take over this pack. Grandpa led like you want too, with kindness, compassion, fairness. Most of the wolves in the pack now don't remember him so they don't know what it was like, I don't actually remember it but grandma told me all about it."

I waited silently, knowing that she wasn't finished speaking and wanting to give her the time she needed to get there.

"He died the year after mom bonded to dad. Left dad as the reigning Alpha and he proved right away he was a mean one. At least, that's what grandma wrote in her journals. She hated that mean streak about him until the day she died. Once she passed, he got worse, it was almost like he was just waiting for her to be gone to show his true colors."

I watched as she ran her fingers across the fireplace mantle, pausing to look at a picture, housed in a decorative silver frame that was sitting in the center. Even in the dark of the house I saw the sad, slow smile ease across Frost's face and I crossed the room and slipped my arms around her waist. I rested my chin on her shoulder as I looked over the picture with her. It was an older print, black and white, slightly yellowed with age and I couldn't help but smile a little at the faces looking out at us. The frame itself was a side by side, hinged in the middle and housing the photo that I was currently looking at and one other.

The left side was the smiling faces of Frost's grandparents, looking happy and completely in love as they held hands, their gazes trained on each other rather than the camera. The right side of the frame was a stunning shot of two wolves, one jet black with a dusting of snow across it's back that I assumed was her grandfather. The other, stark, shocking white with pale eyes that reminded me so much of Frost's wolf it was almost unnerving. The white wolf was nuzzled up under the black wolfs chin, looking as much in an embrace as two standing wolves could. Both photos were heartwarming and I felt a heavy sigh come from the woman in my arms and I tightened my hold on her a bit.

"I wish I'd had the chance to know them, to see what I read in grandma's journals. She wrote about grandpa, the way he led, how much he loved the pack. It always made me proud, then I would remember that my father and brother were power hungry and cruel." She turned in my arms, gave me a small smile before she hugged me and then slipped from my arms and moved to turn on a few lights. "I know you'll love this place, it's beautiful."

"Needs some upgrading but we can get to that later on, I mean it isn't like it's terrible, just a little turn of the century for what we've discussed. Plus, the floor-plan is a little closed off and boxed, I know you like things more open, so do I. Maybe we can knock a couple walls out over the summer while the weather is decent." I turned in a circle, checking the space that I could see and raised an eyebrow when my gaze landed on Frost again and saw the huge grin on her face. "What?"

"I just love the way you've been wording things recently. Like our future together is finally a real thing and we have all the time in the world to make changes that involve things like, well, where we'll be living for the rest of our lives."

I couldn't help but smile back at her and shake my head, she was right, before we had always talked as if the future, our future was some kind of mythical being that we may or may not ever see. Now we were bonded, mated and our future was solid and sealed, definite and I for one couldn't be happier about it.

"Well it's nice to finally know that the future we always hoped for is real. It'll happen and isn't just some distant dream anymore. As long as my father can keep his opinions and his bigotry to himself and stay out of our way. Though I'll be honest, I don't think he has any faith in my ability to lead this pack."

There was no anger or hurt in the words as they left my mouth, I wasn't upset that my father thought I was just some poor, helpless girl and couldn't do anything without a man to head it up. That was just who he was and how he saw the world. The statement was just that, a statement, putting the obvious out there as fact and I didn't let it slow my observation of the kitchen I stepped into. If Frost had something to say on the matter, she kept it to herself and just let me open cabinets and get a feel of what was still in the place and what we would need to look into replacing.

CHAPTER SEVENTEEN

THE NEXT month went by as smoothly as anyone could have expected given the events that had taken place before my return with Frost. We got in touch with a contractor and were in the process of working through plans to renovate her grandparents' house. We had been officially mated with myself installed as Alpha of the Rider pack for a month now and things were strained, but moving forward. I knew we'd have an uphill battle bringing the pack around to our side and our way of thinking, but we would get there. There was a lot of fear and hatred running through this pack. Both of those things had been brought to them through repetition. First by the elder Kendall Alpha and then by his son.

It would take time, patience and understanding to break through the animosity running through these wolves. If there was one thing that I had faith in however, it was that Frost and I had the ability to bring them around to our side, to our way of thinking and doing things. We'd heard a few rumbles from some pack members that would prefer that Freddie take over, that things should continue down the path that Cameron and his father before him had set in motion. While we couldn't understand the desire to continue being beaten down, miserable and treated like nothing more than street mutts we could definitely understand why they wouldn't want us specifically leading the pack. They were threatened by the thought of being led, being ordered around by a couple women, women who were a lot younger than most of them.

I couldn't completely understand the issue there, my age didn't change the fact that I was an Alpha and being a woman didn't diminish my ability to lead. The only part I could follow was on our age, we were both young and the lack of experience could make some of the older members worry. I just had to hope that it would pass eventually. That as we progressed, we would prove ourselves and the pack would be able to see that we could do some good for them. It was a large pack even with the birth rates being so swayed toward the male spectrum in recent years and we knew that full change of mind and pace could take a while.

I was sitting at our small dining table, a mug of steaming coffee in my hands but forgotten as I watched a pair of squirrels play through the trees in the front yard. We had started moving the old furniture around and thinking about replacing some of it once the remodel was finished, which we hoped would be sometime in August. The table I was currently sitting at was admittedly stunning, a dark chocolate-stained four-seat square that looked hand-made and like it was at least a hundred or so years old. Frost had informed me earlier in the month that her grandfather had made the table, and the matching high-backed chairs. I absently ran a fingertip along the rim of the mug as the squirrels flipped, tussled and then charged their way up the massive forty-foot-tall Juniper in the middle of the sprawling front yard.

I couldn't help the little grin that pulled at the corner of my lips, not at the squirrels, but just in general. My life was finally going right, finally looking like the life I had dreamed about since the day I'd gotten involved with Frost. My gaze refocused and the grin I had been wearing faltered at the sight of Greg, one of the former Rider Enforcers that I had relieved of his title for being far too aggressive, striding across the lot toward the house. I let out a heavy sigh and rolled my eyes as I pushed my chair back from the table to stand up, drained my mug and stepped over to the sink to rinse it out. I had just set the rinsed mug in the sink when there was a knock on the door, a heavy-handed one that sounded like anything but someone looking for a polite social call.

I wandered into the living room and toward the front door and heard the shower that had been running upstairs cut off. Frost would be down in a few minutes, I hoped that I could manage to take care of this before she made it to the front of the house. The last thing that I wanted was for her to see more of these ridiculous conversations that never ended well and kept repeating themselves. I had been through this song and dance with Greg a couple times in the last three weeks or so and I was getting tired of it. Not to mention the fact that he couldn't seem to keep it to himself that he had developed quite a liking for my mate. I yanked the front door open and raised an eyebrow at the male standing in front of me, his six-foot-four height meaning that he was nine inches taller than me and I had to look up at him.

"What?"

The word was sharp, clipped and carried all the irritation that I felt for this man that could possibly be forced into a single word. What couldn't be conveyed in the tone was written clearly across my face and Greg actually seemed to take pride in the fact that I was aggravated with him. I wasn't about to let him enjoy this so much so I cleared my expression and managed to put on something that was at least a bit neutral since I couldn't muster a smile.

"Sorry about that, tense morning, a lot going on. What can I do for you Greg?" The more polite greeting seemed to take the wind out of the sail of his ego and he almost looked as though he deflated some, but then recovered.

"I have a bone to pick with you."

"Of course you do. What is it?"

"You've put a serious dent in our enforcers, the pack is starting to feel like we're sitting ducks. We're open to attack like this, you need to reinstate those of us you stripped of our titles, Kyndle."

"No, I don't. Your place and the title that went with it, as well as the places and titles held by Oscar, Parker, Chad and Daniel, were stripped from you for a reason."

"I don't remember being given a reason, at least, not a good one."

"You were given a reason, Greg. Just because you didn't like it doesn't mean it wasn't valid. Enforcers are the protection of the pack, the members we're supposed to look to for comfort, for support and for a safe haven away from the ugly things this world can toss our way. You and the others, you weren't safe for anyone, you were all aggressive, cruel and liked making trouble just so you could be violent. I can't have that in this pack, so I did what I had to do to make sure this pack was safe."

That earned me a glare, but I had said it at least a dozen times to the five men, separately and as a group, over the last month. I was beginning to feel like a broken record, skipping and repeating myself over and over again and it was wearing. I took a moment to let my temper settle, wishing that I wasn't so irritated by this man and his annoying self-righteous attitude that led him to believe that he should get what he wanted just because he wanted it.

I heard a door open upstairs and thanks to the always present heightened werewolf hearing, Greg caught it too. He made a point of shoving past me into the house and I glared at him and bit back a growl that tried to slip free. Snarling and snapping at him wouldn't help me and would only get him riled up and make him confrontational. That was the last thing I needed right now, not that him pushing himself into my house with the hopes of, what? Of seeing or spending a few minutes with my mate? That thought almost brought out that growl again. I had to take a deep breath and force myself to calm down as the barely clad form of my mate appeared from the hallway.

She was wearing a thin pale-gray tee-shirt, her dark

colored bra visible under the fabric and a pair of pale purple girls boxers I'd bought for her while we were in California. Her long, pale legs caught the sunlight as she walked and my eyes narrowed as I watched Greg look her over, a move she didn't notice. My temper flared, but I fought it down, as much as I hated the man, I honestly couldn't exactly blame him for looking, she was gorgeous after all. She was also mine, and I would make sure that he remembered that, I would not let anyone forget it. My gaze slid up her body and I caught her pale hair, still wet from her shower and boasting the slight wave she usually worked out of it when we left the house, framing her face and making those stunning purple eyes pop. My breath caught a little, the anger and frustration I had been feeling a moment earlier at the infuriating man completely shattered. She'd had that effect on me for a while and somewhere deep down I sincerely hoped that it would never stop happening.

"Well hello again, Frost. Tell me honey, when are you gonna get tired of this sad little country girl..." He jerked a thumb over his shoulder at me as he gave her another once over which made her freeze and go a little wide eyed at him. "...and realize you need a man in your life. Someone who can actually take care of you."

My mouth dropped open at the nerve he had talking to her like that and I was about to open my mouth and say something that I might regret later when Frost rolled her eyes at him and pushed past him. She stepped over to me, pressed a quick kiss to my lips and then turned on Greg with a look that I couldn't quite identify.

"That 'sad little country girl' as you called her, is not only my mate but your Alpha Gregory Pine, and you will show her some respect or you'll be dealt with. I can't imagine banishment would look good on you. And for the record, she takes care of me just fine... Better than you could ever hope to."

With that she quirked a pale brow at him, turned on her heel and swept her way into the kitchen, leaving Greg standing there a little shocked at what had just been said to him. It was obvious that he wasn't used to being spoken to in such a way, definitely not by a female ten years his junior and that just made me smirk. My mate was just full of surprises and I could honestly say that I was looking forward to the idea of being surprised for years to come. I stepped over and opened the front door, got Greg's attention with a snap of my fingers and then waved him toward the door. The look he gave me told me that he didn't want to leave and he wasn't ready to drop the conversation yet, if ever.

"I'm not leaving without your word that this will be resolved, Kyndle."

"It has been resolved, Greg. My mind is made up, the decision has been made and the stripping of your places and titles stands. I won't do this again, I'm sick and tired of my authority and choices being questioned and if I catch you or the other former Enforcers here trying to change my mind again I'll banish you from the pack, indefinitely."

CHAPTER EIGHTEEN

A FEW long seconds ticked by, tense and silent and I was starting to think the worst. Greg actually looked like he was about to argue for a split second, but whatever expression crossed my face made him change his mind. His eyebrows dropped into a deep furrow, his eyelids slipping down into a glare and he stormed past me, across the porch and then back out toward the edge of the lot the way he had come from. I wasn't stupid and I knew it wouldn't be the last time I dealt with him or one of the others, and when one of them returned and pushed me I would have no choice but to do just what I'd threatened to do. I shut the door, making sure that I locked it and then made my way into the kitchen to join Frost, taking a few extra moments to just stand in the doorway and stare at her. She felt me standing there and turned away from her coffee that was brewing and smiled at me. Like always, I melted a little.

"So where the hell did that come from?" I asked her.

"Where did what come from?" She asked it so innocently as she turned back to doctor up her now brewed mug of coffee that it was almost believable, if it hadn't been for the sly little smirk on her face.

I grinned and shook my head as I crossed over to her, waited for her to put the mug down and then slapped her smartly on that perfect ass. She yelped, jumping a little as she rounded on me, the most horribly executed mock glare I'd ever seen painted on her face, but the smirk growing.

"You can be a real brat sometimes." I picked up an apple from the fruit bowl on the island counter then turned to lean against the edge as I tossed the piece of fruit back and forth from one hand to the other, grinning at my mate.

"Yeah well, have to keep you on your toes, don't I?" She gave me a wink and then grabbed her coffee, reached around me for the last apple in the bowl and then made her way into the living room. I just watched her walk away, the apple all but forgotten in my left hand as she swayed out of the kitchen like she knew my eyes were focused squarely on the sway of her hips. She probably did know, I had a tendency to stare and she damn well knew that, what an adorable pain in my ass. I chuckled a little and shook my head as I pushed off the counter, dropped the apple back into the bowl and made my way toward the back of the house and upstairs. It was my turn to get ready for the day and that meant getting cleaned up and dressed.

As I walked past the living room and caught sight of Frost stretched out on the couch on her stomach, left leg bent at the knee, foot in the air, one hand in her hair and the other holding open a book she was reading, glasses falling down the bridge of her nose and her shorts riding up a bit, I suddenly needed a very cold shower. I shook myself out of the images that had flooded into my mind and made my way up into the bedroom. It took me all of five minutes to get my clothes for the day together, but then I took a little longer than usual cooling down in my chilled shower. I shivered like mad as I dried off and then slipped into my black skinny jeans, red tank top and matching red chucks. I ran a brush through my towel-dried hair and then let it fall back into place and let it be, it would dry in its own time. I made my way back out into the house, finding Frost right where I'd left her and I attempted to ignore the flaring of heat low in my stomach that the sight of her caused. I collected myself and made my way over to where she was sprawled on the sofa and dropped myself onto her, sitting on her thighs and she laughed and rolled, knocking me onto the floor.

"You mind? I was right in the middle of this chapter."

"Oh I'm sorry, am I distracting you or something?" She narrowed her eyes at me and I burst out laughing at the sight of it, but only because she just couldn't manage to pull it off. She was just too damn sweet to look convincingly ticked off without actually being mad, and that was just too cute. I sat there on the floor and looked at her for a moment and then reached up and gave her a light smack on the thigh. "Come on, we do have things to do today and that means you need to go change."

"Change? You mean I can't go like this?" She feigned shock, her hand on her chest as she looked down at what she was currently wearing and I just let a smirk cross my face.

"Well, I suppose you could but, I'd spend half my day fighting off all the guys staring at you."

I winked at her and she just rolled her eyes, gave the side of my head a light shove and then pushed herself up off the couch and went to change into something she could leave the house in. I pulled myself off the floor, tucked a bookmark between the pages of the book she'd been reading, picked up her apple core and coffee mug and headed back to the kitchen. I left the book on one of the shelves near the door, dropped the apple core in the trash and then rinsed the mug and put it and mine from earlier into the dishwasher before moving back to the living room. I grabbed my keys just as Frost returned from our bedroom in a pair of faded boot-cut jeans, a royal-purple tank top that made her eyes look fierce and black boots. She looked just as amazing as she always did and I gave her a nod toward the front door, popped it open and waited for her to step outside before I followed her.

We loaded up into the car, something that we had decided only days after returning that we needed to have and started off for the day. We had several stops to make, the first being the location that stocked the granite and marble we needed to pick from for the new counters throughout the house. Next was flooring, then cabinets, paint and then the landscapers. Those stops all went over without much issue, just the occasional need for me to raise an eyebrow at a salesman for being a little too friendly with Frost. Once all that was picked out, we made our way back out of town and turned toward Clipper land, and our final stop of the day. We needed to speak with Abbey's parents, something that she had been dreading, but had to be done. She and Kyle were meeting us there, hoping to not only gain Abbey's fathers permission for their bonding but also talk her parents into joining us in rebuilding the Rider pack.

We pulled up to the Simson house and I felt the need to take a moment and collect myself for the meeting that was about to occur. I wasn't afraid of Abbey's parents by any means, I just knew that this could go badly, very badly, the entire meeting and that would crush Abbey. She adored her parents and while I knew that she was going to go through with the bonding with Kyle even if they said they didn't agree with it, she would be hurt if they disapproved of the new relationship. I saw Abbey's truck pull up and gave Frost a small smile before we slipped from our dark blue '79 Camaro. We joined the other couple at the end of the driveway and then the four of us headed for the front door. It opened seconds after Abbey knocked and she was almost immediately pulled into a hug by her mother who was already crying.

"Mom, calm down, I'm fine, seriously." Her mother leaned back when Abbey spoke and just held her at arm's length for a moment before she wiped at her eyes and waved us all into the house. We entered the den of the large house, finding Austin, Abbey's father, sitting in his favorite chair near the fire, empty tumbler in hand. "Hey daddy." Abbey's voice was small, soft and tinged with the nerves and worry she was feeling which caused Kyle to slip an arm around her shoulders. The elder Simson leaned forward in his chair and turned to look at his daughter as a smile crept across his face. He was out of the chair a few moments later and she was out from under Kyle's arm and wrapped up in a hug. Austin gave his daughter a tight squeeze and then released her and nodded in my direction, an action I returned.

"Come on in everyone, sit down, get comfortable. I have the feeling we're in for a bit of a talk, eh?" He glanced from his daughter to me and I just nodded a little in response as we all took seats around the den. Rebecca, Abbey's mother, perched on the arm of her husband's chair, which he returned to, Abbey and Kyle settled on the two-person loveseat and I dropped into the other armchair, Frost nestled in my lap. Austin gave his daughter and this new, unknown male a once over and then glanced at Frost and myself with a raised eyebrow. "So it's true then, the rumor that's been floating around?"

"I can't confirm or deny as I have no idea what you're talking about." I wasn't trying to avoid the conversation. I just legitimately had no clue what he was on about.

"It's going around that you killed Cameron, bonded to his little sister and took over the Rider pack as Alpha."

"Ah that, yes, all very true." I watched as both Austin and Rebecca's faces slipped into expressions of shock and wondered what all was behind the look.

"Well, I guess we just didn't think you had something like that in you. And, well, we had no idea that you were..." Austin trailed off, glanced at his wife and then his daughter as if he wasn't quite sure how to word what it was he wanted to say and I just grinned and shook my head a little.

"Gay?"

"What?"

"You had no idea that I was gay."

"Well, no, we really didn't."

"I know, no one did, not even Abbey. I only told her when I found out my father was forcing the bonding with Cameron. Frost and I were very careful."

He raised an eyebrow at me as if asking what the hell I

was talking about and I remembered that the couple that I had always considered my other parents were confused by my statement.

Frost and I had been dating secretly for about two years before my dad shoved her brother in my face."

This really seemed to shock the pair and the looks on their faces made Abbey burst out laughing before she could catch herself.

"I'm sorry but, you should see your faces. I mean, come on, is it really that hard to believe? I think somewhere deep down I always had an idea that Kyn preferred girls. She just confirmed it."

"What? Oh whatever, we'll talk about that later, right now we're actually here for two reasons and this conversation is not one of them so, let's move on." Everyone nodded in agreement and I glanced over at Abbey and Kyle before I addressed the older couple across from me. "Austin, Becca, first off, I did, in fact, take over the Rider pack and, as Alpha, I asked Abbey to step in as my Beta, and she accepted." This actually seemed like it impressed and excited her father who practically beamed at his little girl with pride. She smiled, brightening almost instantly and I hoped that his reaction to everything else I had to say to him would be even half as positive. "We came here to ask you two things. First, would the two of you consider joining us in the Rider pack? I know it would mean giving up your status here but I was actually considering having co-Betas in the pack. It needs a lot of work and I can't think of any two people better for what I need done than you and Abbey, Austin."

He seemed to be shocked for a moment, then looked as though he was considering the offer and then glanced at his wife and sighed.

"I think you can do a lot of good in that pack Kyndle. Gods know they need it after the two Alpha's they just went through, but I just don't think we can leave. Not because we don't think you have what it takes to lead a pack, I for one believe it completely, but my loyalty, even in hard times, has been to your father and, I can't abandon him, or the pack, now."

It hurt to hear that but I understood completely, even if I had been hoping he would drop everything and help us out. I knew he and my father had been friends for years before he and my mother had bonded, he remembered the man Dane used to be and probably hoped he'd see him again one day.

"I understand. Just know that the offer stands if you ever change your mind. You always have a place with us."

I glanced at Frost for confirmation and she gave them a nod and a smile to back up what I had said and I grinned at her. While I was taking the leading role as far as the face of the pack went, Frost and I really were a team, leading together, making choices as a pair rather than one of us just rolling over and letting the other make the decisions. It was a deal that we had made when we had first found out that I would have to kill her brother and would be taking over the pack. I knew she would be by my side and I wanted her to have a say in how the pack she had grown up in was ruled. Austin and Rebecca seemed to be genuinely thankful for the offer but Austin was soon ready to know what else we were there for.

"What's your other reason?"

"I think I'll hand this one off to Abbey..." I shot my best friend a look and she smiled, but then took a deep breath and steadied herself for what she was about to say.

"Dad, mom, I know I don't really need you to okay this, but I'm asking anyway. Kyle asked me to be his mate, we'd like you to bless the bonding." Austin took a moment to let what his daughter, his only child, had just asked him sink in and then he set his glass down and looked over at Kyle.

"How old are you son?"

"Just turned twenty-seven."

Austin nodded a little at the response and I wondered for a moment what he thought of his baby girl with a male that was not only from another pack but was also nine years her senior.

"Beta?"

"Yes, sir. Mother, father and brother are both co-Betas in other packs."

"Good, good. No delusions of grandeur? Not interested in shoving my girl out of her place as Beta? Or my other girl out as Alpha?" I beamed a little at that, glad to hear that he counted me as an unofficial daughter as much as I counted him my second dad.

"None at all, sir. They're both more dominant than I am and I'm perfectly okay with that. My mother is her packs first Beta, dad is technically co-Beta, but he really just backs her up. So it's how I grew up. Normal for me sir." Austin nodded again and gave himself a few moments to digest this information and then looked to his wife again before turning his attention back to us.

"Well I've always been proud of my judgment of character and you seem like a decent sort, Kyle. I'll agree to blessing this bonding if you promise me you won't break my girls heart." Kyle and Abbey both smiled as Kyle nodded vigorously in agreement with the lines drawn out for him.

"Of course, sir. I wouldn't ever do anything to hurt Abbey, I adore her. Thank you, sir."

Abbey couldn't contain herself anymore, she leaped from the chair and practically pounced on her father, hugging him tightly. She turned her attention on her mother next, holding the older woman close for a few seconds before she returned to Kyle and jumped into his arms. I couldn't help but laugh a little at her, she was so excited that she was acting like she'd just won the lottery and I couldn't blame her one bit. It was good to see her so happy and I knew that she wanted a big, blowout of a bonding ceremony, which I was about to be forced into helping her plan. Oh, yay.

Chapter Nineteen

The weather had shifted from the wet days of spring into the heat of summer and plans for Abbey and Kyle's bonding ceremony were well underway. I had always preferred the dead of winter over the summer months, but for once I welcomed July like I never had before. Having Frost by my side seemed to make it all just a little easier to handle, even though the renovations on the house were well underway and the place was a complete mess. I stepped over the cord for one of the saws the crew was using, not even sure what this particular one was for and shook my head. I couldn't wait for the remodel to be finished so we could have our home back, it had barely even had the chance to actually feel like home before all the chaos began. I pulled the sliding door open and stepped out into the backyard to join Frost who was lounging by our new pool. That had been finished rather quickly since we insisted on having it completed for the summer months. The crew had busted their butts to get it done and we loved it.

"Hey you." Frost turned to smile up at me when I spoke and pulled off her sunglasses as I dropped down onto the lounge chair beside her.

"Hey yourself." I grinned back at her when she answered

me and leaned back against the backrest of the chair. I closed my eyes as I listened to the crew inside return from their lunch break and get back to work. "I'm so glad that they finished the pool first."

"Oh gods, me too. It's been nice already, I can't wait to get more use out of it." I nodded in agreement and then let out a sigh, taking a moment to just relax since those were few and far between these days. If it wasn't one thing it was another lately and if it wasn't something in the house that needed a last-minute change or upgrade it was Freddie pulling one of his stunts, which were getting really old. It had been almost a week since he'd stormed onto the property and made a scene and he was, if his pattern held, due for another any time now. I didn't want to alienate the part of the pack that was loyal to that part of the family, banishing that many wolves at one time was detrimental to the pack as a whole.

I was rapidly approaching the point where I wouldn't have a choice however, I could only take his ego and insubordination for so long before it became an issue of hierarchy and respect. Not to mention the fact that the mutinous attitude that he was brewing in the outliers within the pack was going to start getting dangerous.

"Well don't you two just look like the picture of relaxation out here." I was so lost in thought that I hadn't even realized that Abbey and Kyle had been standing there for the last minute or so. I popped one eye open and looked over at my best friend with a grin as Frost just chuckled at her and stretched lazily. I sat up, stretched and let out a yawn before I patted the chair beside me and Abbey took the space, leaving Kyle to sit beside Frost once she sat up and resettled herself as well.

"So, we've got a good chunk of everything decided on, we just have to figure out where this thing is happening and who all is being invited."

I nodded to that and chewed on my lower lip a little, that was the big issue, who all to invite since there would obviously be members of the Clipper pack that would want to attend.

I wasn't about to tell Abbey that our former classmates and her buddies from her old job couldn't come to her bonding. I also wasn't completely stupid, I knew that there was a lot of tension right now, not only between the two packs thanks to my confrontation with my father, but also within the packs themselves. The Riders were split between loyalty to Freddie, their former Alpha's uncle, and a sense of duty and honor toward me, their new Alpha. Meanwhile, the Clippers were split between their loyalty to my father as their Alpha and their understanding that pack law stated that taking over the Rider pack was my right.

It was a case of being caught between a rock and a hard place in each pack and it was stressing me out. Which was exactly why I had been attempting to relax by my newly-added pool, to de-stress a little bit, hopefully. I came back to the conversation just as Abbey mentioned something about making me wear a chartreuse dress and I looked at her like she was the embodiment of all that was dark and evil.

"Oh my gods you should see your face right now, Kyndle!" She was laughing so hard that her eyes were watering and I responded by shoving her hard enough that she fell sideways off the lounger. That made the other three of us burst out laughing as she sat up and glared at me before starting up again herself.

"That wasn't nice you know."

"Well, that'll teach you to zone out when I'm talking to you! I should put you in one just for revenge now."

"Don't. You. Dare. I swear to all that is right and holy that I will murder you in your sleep Abigail Simson." That made her laugh even harder, so hard that she actually let out a little snort, which set the rest of us off again.

I had to admit that it felt good to be sitting here, at home, beside my pool with my mate, my best friend and her future mate, laughing like a bunch of hyenas about absolutely nothing. We all needed it more than we would ever let on, definitely Frost and Abbey who had been dealing with my moodiness the last few weeks. They each deserved a damn medal for their efforts and I would have to find a way to make sure I thanked them each properly for all their love and support once things calmed down. Thanking Abbey would be the difficult task, she could be a bit of a pain to do anything nice for, tough to shop for and almost impossible to surprise. Frost, however, would be significantly easier to thank properly and I was definitely looking forward to that particular thank you.

"What are you smirking at over there?" Kyle's voice dragged me from the rather dirty images that had started flickering through my mind and I glanced between the three of them quickly, my cheeks flushing slightly when my eyes met Frost's.

"Oh gods, Kyndle, seriously? Are you just, like, always... On... These days?" Abbey threw her arms in the air in mock exasperation and Kyle took a second to process then burst out laughing, their recognition of what I'd been thinking sending Frost into a full-blown blush. "Awww, we embarrassed Frost. Sorry sweetie."

Sorry, she said it but we all knew she didn't mean it. This was Abbey and any chance that she had to embarrass the living hell out of one of us was taken and well used. I rolled my eyes as Abbey launched into another fit at Frost's suddenly-deepened blush. She was such a pain sometimes. I glanced over at my mate and gave her a smile and a little wink, which seemed to help a little, but then turned my gaze on my best friend, and shoved her right off the chair again. We laughed so hard our eyes watered and all our cheeks and stomachs started to hurt, it felt wonderful.

"What a picture of leadership, we should all be so proud of our Alpha." The voice cut off the laughter instantly as we all turned to look at the last person we had wanted to see that day. Freddie stood there looking rather smug, as per usual, his arms crossed over his chest as he attempted to be intimidating.

"You know, Freddie, I'm getting really tired of you treating this house like it's your own personal getaway. You need to learn to knock, or at least let us know you're coming."

"You want respect then?" I just raised an eyebrow at him, accompanied by a look that rather clearly stated 'yeah stupid, get the memo already'. "Well, little she-wolf, respect is earned. Earn it and I'll bother to show it."

My temper flared and my blood boiled, but the only outward sign of it was the slight ring of red that rimmed my ice blue irises. I kept myself in check as I stood, the movement controlled, deliberate, until I was on my feet facing the rude male.

"Get out, Freddie."

He planted his feet shoulder width apart and quirked a dark brow at me, a clear sign that he wasn't leaving, that he was, once again, defying me. I was getting really tired of letting these moments of ego slide and it was time to land him squarely in his place, right on his ass. I very calmly closed the gap between us, cocked my head just slightly to the right as if studying him, smirked and then dropped a little, kicked my right leg out and swept his legs right out from under him. I was too quick for him to catch the move coming and he ended up on his back beside the pool, shock written clearly across his features. His brows furrowed down and his gaze dropped into a glare as he registered what I had just done and he went to get to his feet. I wasn't about to let that happen and, once again in a move that he was a little too slow to counter, I planted a sneaker-clad foot against his neck.

"Big mistake little gir~"

I wasn't about to let him insult me, not ever again and definitely not in my own home and I cut him off by pressing my shoe down into his neck.

"Stop talking, Freddie, and just listen. I'm sick and tired of your ego and your refusal to back down. You may have been Beta for this pack once, but even then you weren't worthy of that title. Cameron let you have it because he didn't want a Beta who would continue to challenge him, who would speak up when he did something stupid. He terrified you and you kept your mouth shut, that's what he wanted. I didn't want to have to resort to anger and aggression to make you behave, but apparently that's all you know how to pay attention to. This is your last warning Freddie. You are not my Beta, you never will be, you are little better than an Omega with a god-complex and I won't have you testing and questioning my authority anymore. You will show me some respect, as your Alpha, or next time, I won't bother to banish you. I'll kill you. Am I making myself clear?"

He seemed to take a moment to decide if I was being serious, not looking like he believed me so I leaned down, resting my arm on the knee of the foot on his neck and pushed down a little. Anger flashed in my eyes, the red ring growing and almost eclipsing the blue of my irises and I saw his eyes go wide. "Am. I. Clear. Freddie?" I punctuated each word with a growl that deepened with every pause and I actually heard his breath catch as he rushed to nod. For the first time since I'd shown up after defeating Cameron, Freddie was scared of me and what I might do. He had reason to be. I wasn't the type of Alpha that enjoyed violence, but I was still an Alpha and I would do what I had to do to maintain my place, my respect and the safety of my new pack. I let him up, straightened then crossed my arms over my chest and watched as he scrambled to his feet and bolted from the yard. With any luck at all, that would be the last issue that we had with Freddie, though I was only on so-so terms with my luck these days, it seemed to have a sick and twisted sense of humor.

"Damn." That single word was all I heard from the three wolves behind me, Kyle's voice tinged with both respect and a little fear. Abbey just let out a low whistle and Frost grinned at me like a proud wife, I admit, I liked that look on her. I quirked a cinnamon-colored brow at them and shrugged as if asking them what the hell they were all staring at.

"That was terrifying... Seriously Kyndle, for a kinda average sized chick, you're scary as hell."

I studied him for a moment, making him shuffle from foot to foot nervously and look at the pavement below his feet before I burst out laughing. Abbey snorted a little as Kyle's gaze shot up and moved between us and then he huffed, threw his arms in the air and grinned before shoving Abbey into the pool, fully-clothed. I went wide eyed for a second, watched her surface and then fell apart and started laughing all over again. Kyle jumped in after Abbey, also still fully clothed and I just shook my head as I watched them splash each other and squeal like they were twelve.

"It's kinda sexy watching you go all power Alpha on someone..." The goofy grin was stripped off my face in that one sentence from my mate, whispered in my ear as she slid her arms around my waist. I laid my left hand on her arms at my waist and wrapped my right hand up around the back of her neck as I turned my head to look at her.

"Oh really?" She simply gave a quick quirk of her right brow and then smirked at me and kissed the tip of my nose then leaned her forehead against mine.

"Really..." The single word was barely audible as she whispered it against my lips and I felt my knees go a little weak with the rush of warmth from her breath across my skin.

"Seriously? Guys, I'd say get a room but you already have one, about seventy feet that way." Abbey interrupted the moment and I turned to glare at her, which prompted her to throw a beach ball at me. I threw it back and she ducked just in time for it to miss her head then let out a loud 'HA' seconds before I was pushed into the pool. I knew before I even broke the surface of the water that my sweet mate had been the one to give me the push, and she was so going to get it for that. I came up a few seconds later, took a deep breath and hauled myself out over the side, Frost standing there grinning at me and biting back a laugh. I smiled sweetly at her as I walked over and wrapped my arms around her, my jeans and tank top soaked through as I dripped all over the pavement.

"You're gonna get it for that love." I whispered in her ear as I hauled her up over my shoulder and then rather unceremoniously tossed her right into the pool. She hit the bottom, planted her feet and pushed back to the surface, breaking it in a spray of water that made Abbey turn her head to keep from getting water in her eyes.

"That wasn't very nice." She pouted at me and I just laughed a little, leaned over and offered her my hand to help her out of the pool. She ducked under the water and swam over to the edge I was standing on, surfaced right in front of me and reached for my hand. "Turn-about is fair play, sweetheart." I barely had time to register her whisper before she yanked my hand, pulling me off my feet and landing me headfirst in the pool, again. I came up and was laughing again moments after breaking the surface, feeling all the tension from earlier slipping completely away. Sometimes I seemed to forget that Abbey, Frost and I were only eighteen, all the stress, complication and chaos we had been through making us all feel, and seem, older.

It was nice to get to act our ages for a little while, forget that we had serious things to deal with that had to be handled delicately. I still wondered if I had what it took to lead sometimes. Not that I ever said it out loud, just let it wander through my head at night after Frost had fallen asleep and I was alone with my thoughts. Eventually we would develop a mental connection and there wouldn't be any of that, she would catch them unless I worked hard to shut her out. Since I couldn't imagine doing that she would know everything. Not being sure how to bring it up to her was one thing, but actually intentionally shutting her out wasn't something I could ever see myself doing.

We spent the next couple hours goofing off and just acting like a bunch of kids before we finally removed ourselves from the pool, dried off, redressed and settled in to discuss serious matters. "You aren't really gonna make me wear chartreuse, are you?" I was toweling the last dredges of pool water from my hair as best I could as I eyed Abbey, hoping she'd been joking. She made a face and shook her head, showing that she didn't even want to look at the color, not enough to make me wear it anyway.

"Thank the gods. What about the dress thing, do I really have to wear a dress?"

"Yes, Kyn, you really have to wear a dress." I looked at her stunned as my jaw dropped a little, I seriously thought she'd been jerking my chain when she'd said I'd be wearing a dress for this thing.

"Seriously? Oh Abs, come on! You know I don't do dresses!"

"I know you don't Kyndle but this is my bonding ceremony, the only one I'll ever have and, frankly, I'd like to see you in one. Besides, I think Frost deserves to see you in a dress at least once, don't you?" I looked at Frost, hoping that she would have my back on this matter, she knew how much of a tomboy I was.

"You do have really nice legs babe. I'd love to see you all dressed up." She beamed at me, actually looking forward to seeing me all dolled up and looking like a girl and it melted my resolve.

"Okay, fine. You win." Her smile brightened and Abbey stuck her tongue out at me and put on a rather impressive, but very fake, pout. "What?"

"Won't do it for me, your best friend, when it's my ceremony... But you'll do it for Frost, eh?"

"Yep. Sounds about right."

"Boo... Why?"

"Ask me that again if it's ever you I'm having sex with." I shot her a wink and she rolled her eyes then smiled at me, probably having figured I'd say something like that.

"Well hot damn, make sure I'm home if that ever happens!"

I gave Kyle a 'you did not just say that' look and he and Abbey both burst out laughing at me, Frost biting her lower lip to keep from joining them.

"You should see your face baby. You're paler than me."

I was stunned, that's what I was, which had apparently drained all the color from my face as I sat there and shook my head.

"And for the record, Kyle... Never happening. I like Abbey, but I'd seriously have to kill her." Frost kept her tone light but she was dead serious as she walked over when I settled into one of the armchairs and folded herself into my lap. "Mine." The single syllable came out as a soft growl as she wrapped her arms around my waist and rested her head against my neck. I just grinned like an idiot, still loving it every time she got all possessive like that and pretty sure I'd always love it.

"Yes, yours. And no worries, I wouldn't let it happen anyway." Abbey stuck her tongue out at me which earned her a goofy face and we laughed for a minute and then settled back into plans for the ceremony. Eventually we ended up on the topic of dealing with who to invite and where to host it. "Let's just have it here guys."

"I agree, might as well. Our backyard runs right up to the woods a couple acres back and it's stunning out here at night. Plus, we have more than enough space for a big group." I smiled at Frost and then looked over at Abbey and Kyle expectantly, it really did make sense and they agreed after talking it over for a moment.

"Good, with that taken care of, on to guest list. Look, Abbey, this is gonna be about you so, I say you invite whoever the hell you want from the old pack. An invite will go to our entire pack with the option to attend if wanted, but with the express instructions that it will be a confrontation-free event. Anyone gets weird or mean and I'll toss them out myself, dress or no dress."

That made Abbey and Frost both grin and then everyone nodded in agreement that the plan sounded like it would work as long as everyone could keep their panties from getting in a bunch for a couple hours.

"What about the run after?" I looked at my mate and thought about it for a moment then sighed and looked at Kyle and Abbey across from us.

"Everyone can run if they'd like, but the same rules apply. Any fighting and I'll step in and handle it myself."

They all nodded again and with the major points finally agreed on, our friends decided to head back to the house we had set them up in. Once we had said our goodbyes and I was alone with Frost again we wandered into our kitchen and looked around. It was still a mess and probably would be for a few more weeks but it was already beginning to come together. We chatted about the progress the crew had made the last few days and looked over what they still needed to finish for a bit. I had just stepped into the downstairs bedroom they were remodeling and started looking around when I felt her arms around me. I leaned back into her and rested my head against her cheek with a smile as my hands found hers. "This room will look nice once it's done."

"Mmhmm... Not really the room I'm interested in at the moment though." Her voice was soft in my ear and held the tinge of something I knew all too well that made my breath catch and left heat flooding my body. I didn't speak, just slipped her arms from around me, took her hand and led her to the only room she had on her mind just then, our bedroom. The short walk was filled with memories of times when I had been the one to try and push things too far and she'd had to slow it down and tell me we needed to wait. I couldn't help but smile as I thought back on those days, the nights I laid awake alone in my bed and wondered if she really did like girls. Wondered if she wanted me as much as I wanted her, not sure since she was always putting the brakes on. How things had changed since then as now she was the aggressor and instigator just as often as I was. She had more than proven over the last three months since we'd bonded how much she really did want me and I loved the way it made me feel.

CHAPTER TWENTY

MORNING THE day of Abbey's ceremony came far too soon for my liking, probably because Frost had kept me engaged in activities that actively kept sleeping at bay until well after three in the morning. She was damn good at that, not that you would catch me complaining about it, ever, for any reason. I growled at the alarm clock and seriously considered throwing the damned thing across the room but just as I was about to grab for it, Frost rolled over, reached across me and shut it off. I grinned a little at the feel of her weight on top of me, the offending clock already completely forgotten to my often-one-track mind. "Mmm, well good morning gorgeous." I practically purred the words at her as I ran my hands up her back and then down her sides and she looked down at me and rolled her eyes.

"Don't start you."

"Start? Me? Never. I'm not starting anything. You're the one who decided to lay on top of me all naked and sexy first thing in the morning." I let my hands drift toward her hips and she reached down and swatted at me before she rolled to the other side of the bed and slipped from under the blankets.

"You are completely insufferable. We have to get ready,

Abbey will have both our heads if we're late. So get your head out of the gutter and focus woman." I let out a soft growl in her direction as she walked across our bedroom to the closet, still completely naked, making it very hard to think of anything but her. "Now, Kyndle. I'm all yours after the run tonight, but at the moment, get your cute perverted little butt out of bed and get dressed." I couldn't help but giggle at her and finally forced myself out of the bed and into a pair of jeans and a tank top. The clothes we would be wearing for the ceremony were at Abbey's place and we would be changing there after helping her get ready. Dressed and ready to go we put some coffee together in our travel mugs and headed down the street, our destination only about seven houses down.

It took us all day to handle Abbey, first calming her nerves and getting her to sit still for five minutes so the poor girl doing her hair could work and then doing the same again for makeup. We finally managed to get her into her dress and I had to admit, my best friend looked stunning, treating her ceremony like a wedding. She was in a pure white dress, something that I had teased her about endlessly since she had Kyle had already been living together for well over five months. I didn't know much about dresses but Frost had helped me make sense of everything each of us would be wearing that day. Abbey's was backless, showing off the crescent moon tattoo she had gotten between her shoulder blades to piss her mom off when we were sixteen. It had wide straps but was sleeveless, perfectly fitted to her hips and then flared out like any good wedding dress should be, at least, that's what she'd said.

Frost got ready next and, thankfully, Abbey wasn't making us wear any shade of red or green, she had actually chosen a deep, midnight blue that made Frost's eyes looking shockingly lavender and mine pop like glacial ice. My mate looked amazing and it took a few minutes for she and Abbey to get me to pay attention enough to make me go put my own dress on. I felt ridiculous in the thing but I had promised them both that I would wear it and not complain about it, much. I worked myself into it and then called Abbey in to zip it up and she was shocked for a moment, but then recovered and helped me finish with it.

"Frost is gonna flip when she sees you, Kyn. You look... Wow." With that she gave me another quick look, shook her head and grinned as she left the room to let me take my time getting used to the damned thing. I didn't want to look, but I had to see what I had gotten myself into, what she had seen, what Frost would be seeing in a couple minutes when I stepped out so I turned toward the full-length mirror. The dress was tailored to fit and hugged every curve I had just right, the deep blue sharpening the color of my hair and making it look more red. It was strapless, with what Frost had called a 'sweetheart' neckline, which made total sense now that I was staring at it, and fell to about two inches above my knees. The outfit was completed by shoes in a matching color with a two-inch heel on them which I was sure I would trip in and break something.

I thought I looked totally insane, but it was time to see what everyone else thought so I took a deep breath and stepped out of the room. Abbey smiled at me and then tapped Frost on the shoulder to get her attention away from Rebecca. She glanced at Abbey, who pointed toward me and my mate followed her finger, turning to take me in. I waited, holding my breath, just knowing that someone was about to laugh at me, knowing I had to look as awkward as I felt. Abbey just slipped her hand onto her mother's arm and grinned at me, allowing Frost and I to have this moment despite it being her day. She was really a great friend.

I watched as Frost froze, her eyes going wide as her mouth dropped open a little and I waited for her to giggle at me. She didn't, instead she stood there, silent and staring at me, not making a sound and it started to make me uncomfortable. Abbey reached over and poked her in the shoulder, snapping her out of it and back to the room with us and she just smiled at me. "My god... Kyndle. Damn."

"Should have made her wear a dress for your ceremony,

huh?" Frost just nodded and finally moved, taking the few steps toward me and wrapping her arms around my neck.

"You look gorgeous baby." She was a little breathless and I could feel her heart pounding in her chest as she hugged me close, racing so fast anyone would have sworn she'd been running. Well, at least she liked it and from the all too familiar scent that hit me a second later, we might not make it home after the run, or even to the run itself, before she made good on her promise from that morning. I grinned and hugged her back tightly before we turned all of our attention back to Abbey for the rest of the evening. We filed out to where we would be entering the yard from and saw Kyle already standing near the arch we had set up. Chairs were filled with members from both packs and it was full, everyone Abbey had invited having shown as well as a few extras.

The ceremony went off without a hitch, Frost and Abbey cried openly and I did my best to pretend that I wasn't, but failed. Once the bonding part was complete, we all milled around, chatted, danced and ate and waited for the sun to finish setting. Once the moon was up, members from both packs headed for the tree line at the back of our property and started stripping out of their clothes. One by one, shifting began and in a matter of moments the run was underway, yips and howls filling the mid-September air around us. We ran together for well over an hour and then finally everyone headed back to the house, shifted back and started slipping back into clothes. Once dressed, pack members from both sides congratulated the happy couple again and then made toward their homes. Roughly half the guests had left when I heard a familiar voice from across the yard and stopped right in the middle of a sentence as I was speaking to Talia, one of the Clipper girls we had gone to school with.

I turned and made my way across the space, closing the gap between myself and my target with Abbey, Kyle and Frost on my heels. Austin and Rebecca weren't far behind them but kept back far enough to not be in the way of whatever might be about to happen. A yelp broke the silence that had fallen in the open space and then a whine as fist met face before I jumped between the two individuals. "Stop it!"

"Get out of my way, Kyndle!"

"No. Leave him alone." I had planted myself firmly between my father and his target, my brother, Shane.

"He disobeyed a direct order and it's my right as his Alpha to punish him. Now move!" My father was livid and I knew why, he had forbidden my mother and brothers, as well as my two oldest brothers' mates and children, from attending the ceremony. Shane and I had always been fairly close with only thirteen months separating us and he had chosen to defy our father and attend anyway. He may have been a year older than me, but it was painfully obvious in that moment that Shane had never been the Alpha wolf the rest of us in the family were.

"Yes he did, and that may be but you will not do it here."

"Watch me. Move."

"No. This is my territory and you won't touch him as long as he's here. I made it clear that violence would not be tolerated tonight."

"Your territory. Ha! By default, by luck. Shane, let's go, we'll finish this at home." Shane whined and looked up at me and my heart broke a little for him and his situation, I knew my father's temper too well. I offered Shane my hand and he took it, standing up to his full height, at least four inches taller than me, but staying behind me for safety.

"He's not going anywhere tonight. He's staying with us. If you're still angry at him tomorrow, come to the house and we'll discuss him returning to Clipper land. Until then, please leave." Something in my father's eyes flashed and I watched as the civility drained from him in a matter of seconds.

"There will be no discussion. You've gone too far this time, Kyndle. I'm tired of you meddling and getting in the way. You don't belong here, leading this pack, no female does."

"You may believe that, but it's mine all the same."

ABOUT THE AUTHOR

Kaden is an Arizona based author currently living north of Phoenix with her wife and small zoo of pets. She loves all things nerdy and can regularly be found playing board and table top games, writing new D&D campaigns, browsing through the nearest convention or listening to true crime podcasts.

Conquest: Kai's Story
2017 Rainbow Awards Honorable Mention

"This story is extremely well written, the plot flows effortlessly, it made me feel, the characters come to life, I hated having to put it aside to get on with real life. In short, Conquest ticked all the boxes that make a book a top-notch read for me." - Dee England

In the late 24th century, life seemed to be going well for the human population of Earth. War, famine, debt, and disease had been eradicated and a new era of peace and discovery was ushered in. However, as history has taught us over and over again, there is rarely a rise without a corresponding fall.

When a new technology which brought free, clean energy to all of mankind failed, the planet and its human population suffered great loss. With most of the people once inhabiting the planet dead or dying, a new time of human rose to the place of survival: the Regen. Able to use the deadly radiation leaked into Earth's flora, fauna, and atmosphere as a healing agent, the Regens constantly regenerate their cell structure. The result is a lack of radiation-caused disease and lengthened lifespans.

However, each and every human being must have its opposite and for the Regens this meant the Purists. Average humans who were somehow immune to radiation poisoning and other effects. Taking up their side against the Regens and labeling them evil, a new era of struggle, powerplays, and fighting dawned.

Follow four Regen Resistance Generals in their quest to be named as equals to the Purists. Each General, giving a nickname by the Purist leaders, represents one of the Four Horsemen of the Apocalypse. Meet Kai, known by her enemies as Conquest, in this first installment of a set of four novels.

Silver Linings and Angel Wings

In a world where Vampires reign and humans have two purposes, food or entertainment, can a human woman hope to become more than someone's next meal?

Enter the world of the Vampire Elite, a High Council of ruling Vampires who govern the world from their own blood-driven perspective. Silver, the daughter of their leader, Ayana and her Lycan mate Ianos is the world's first and only hybrid. She's also the future leader of the Council. With a chip on her shoulder which competes with the expanse of her mother's sizeable territory and a disdain for human life, she is frequently the cause of problems within their ranks.

When she finds herself sharing space with a human woman who isn't afraid of her, who challenges her at every turn, how will she react? Will her mounting confusion about her connection to the human tear apart her last strand of self-control? Most importantly, can a hybrid who has always hated humans ever learn to love one? All these questions send ripples through Silver's life when Angel enters the picture, turns her world upside down and makes her feel things she never thought possible.

"Not for long." With that, he turned on his heel and stormed away from the house, heading back toward his own border and onto his own land. I knew he would be back. What he had just said was as good as a challenge for my position as Alpha. My father wanted my new pack, and he would kill me to get it.